Hall   c.2
    I like it better now.

DATE DUE

I LIKE IT BETTER NOW

JAMES B. HALL

THE UNIVERSITY OF ARKANSAS PRESS
FAYETTEVILLE   1992

C . 2

Save for the final story these short fictions first appeared in the following magazines: "The Lettuce Wars" in *Interim;* "The Rock Pool" in *West Coast Review;* "In the Valley of the Kilns" in *Omni Magazine;* "Inside a Budding Grove" and "In the Eye of the Storm" in the *San Francisco Review;* "The Snow Hunters" in *Quarry West #19;* "I Like It Better Now" in *Atlantic Monthly;* "Confessions of Friday" in *Georgia Review/ New Directions Anthology #45;* and "A Rumor of Metal" in *Castle Peak Editions.* All are reprinted here with permission.

"How Old Man Found What Was Lost" (originally, "Old Man Finds What Was Lost"), "A Circle of Friends," and "Beirut" first appeared in *New Letters* (50:4, Summer 1984), *New Letters* (52:1, Fall 1985), and *New Letters* (55:1, Fall 1988), respectively. They are reprinted here with the permission of *New Letters* magazine and the Curators of the University of Missouri-Kansas City.

"But Who Gets the Children" was first published in *Esquire,* June 1960; reprinted with permission, courtesy of the Hearst Corporation.

In many instances, for this collection, these stories have been revised or virtually rewritten and thus stand in their imagined final form.

Library of Congress Cataloging-in-Publication Data

Hall, James B.
    I like it better now: short stories/by James B. Hall.
      p.   cm.
    ISBN 1-55728-233-1 (cloth). — ISBN 1-55728-234-X (paper)
    I. Title.
PS3558.A368I2   1992
813'.54--dc20
                                      91-18714
                                         C I P

For Bill and Judy Hotchkiss, in all affection

Contents

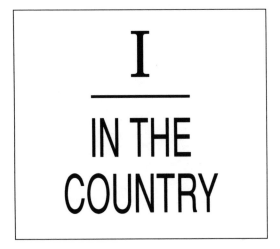

I

IN THE COUNTRY

The Lettuce Wars

Paco said everyone in that work miss sometime, but I think not that Sparger, that one pilot all the time up north in Nam, flying now Con-Ag's Swearingen, firewall her, war-max, on spray, on duster runs, on all applications, on the deck then pullllup. *Over* all power lines. Hey, you Blue-Leader One!

Oh, that Sparger. When my lettuce crew is down, I mess around their Con-Agra strip: one chopper, two Stearman, one Swearingen, Ag-stressed. Once I touched the cowling. Smooth, cold, just when Mr. Sparger saw me and laugh:

"Hey, Jose! That airplane will eat your lunch."

Now, out of the mist, *under* the wires, like knocking gooks in Nam, I saw sun-glare on the canopy. *Hit* the deck, my two lettuce rows. I looked up, into his prop.

Ahead, one wing hit dirt. Then our truck wheel.

The Swearingen did one big cartwheel. Bounced. Then it came apart, dust bins let go. White poison dust went up. Settled, and Oh, broth-er, bought a farm, like Nam.

"Gasleen fire!" Paco yelled, but I crawled under the upside-down wing folded back. Not Sparger. Maybe the Stearman guy.

No gasleen fire. I hope.

Some pilot was hanging upside down inside the cockpit braces, but still aimed down my two rows.

Paco also crawled underneath behind me, "Cut too close. One time."

Inside the crash it was metal and dirt and lettuce and oil twisted everywhere.

"Maybe burn," Paco said, then yelled loud, NO SMOKING!

I pulled one piece of metal out of the helmet. Then I got loose the strap, not move the pilot's head, pull off his blue, very warm crash helmet.

And Oh, brother. Sparger, Blue-Leader One. All fucked up.

Through little tunnels of light, all around the crash, I saw shoes and boots and pant legs walking around and around. Everyone kicking the dirt, saying how they saw everything, and also afraid of maybe fire.

Paco squirmed in beside me. Very close he looked Mr. Sparger face, said, "Leave him upside down. Never move an injured man. Okay?"

We all know that.

Paco crawled back out under the wing and told everyone for sure: Sparger was the pilot.

I stayed inside. Now his face was very white, also covered with ag-dust, except his hair where the helmet had covered; his hair was wet, grey.

No one else crawled in so I watched him and one time touched his hair, said, "Okay, okay, now we no burn."

Afterwards, Roy, our team's Number Two, said, "He chop."

Afterward, I said, "Shit:

"I saw right up into his prop. He firewalled it, like going north in Nam. Hauled ass. Sparger *handling* that Swearingen. No pilot error, man. Maybe mag-drop, maybe no vac boost. Or sun got him. He saw it. Just too late. Hey, Mr. Sparger, he *fly* that thing."

Roy said, "Hey boy, just *one* time miss in that work."

Everybody from all the fields that saw it stood around. Some say bad, a bad one. But no gasleen fire, and that's good. Others say now Con-Ag sells one airplane to the insurance company, and no one on the ground got hit and that's good.

I looked down and saw my own hand still holding the piece of metal I pulled from his helmet.

Soon the ambulance came, red lights tilting like a boat's lights across our lettuce rows.

When the doors opened the bed came out. Then another man not wearing a white jacket came out and he climbed up on the roof of the ambulance.

Also another man not wearing a white jacket got out and handed up a TV camera, the shoulder kind.

Roy said, "Now everybody on TV. Show respect."

The ambulance had no doctor—only a tec.

The tec and Paco followed me back under the wing. The tec looked up at him, Mr. Sparger, still hanging upside down.

Right then I saw this tec don't understand a buckle or shoulder straps.

"No way," Paco told him, "that way he falls. Upside down. Break his neck, if not already done that job."

The tec said, "He's fucked up bad. Maybe lower him."

Uncle Paco and me got a hold.

The tec let go all the straps.

Now lower. Low-er. Ea-sy—

Mr. Sparger was very soft inside his coveralls. We

easy slide him out of the cockpit cage and out—easy, boys—beneath the wing.

Outside, they put Mr. Sparger on the bed and tightened the white straps, did not even listen to his heart, or anything. Their blanket had a blue border, the hospital kind, and they covered Mr. Sparger's face.

"We can't pronounce in the field," the ambulance driver told Roy, "but he's a goner."

"No pronounce dead?"

"Only a doctor can pronounce. But he's out of it. A real fatal crash."

A TV cameraman come down now off the ambulance roof.

"Got my footage," he told the ambulance driver.

With no siren and no lights the ambulance headed for the gate, and then the paved road to Watsonville.

Everybody picked up loose pieces, stacked them. Tomorrow or the next day the insurance people will get here from District.

For all lettuce crews it's over.

"Cut lettuce," Paco told Number Two Man and me, his Number Four Man.

We cut and grade and pack off the platform: one head of lettuce in the air at all times.

If Paco grades out a head, it's bad. No need to check it. Then out lettuce hauls ass, firewall it to Boston or Miami, in Florida. Our team roll it fast, get paid per box.

Roy said, "Man just killed."

Paco said, "Everyone saw it," and turned to our rig. Like go.

Roy looked down his rows, maybe saw a grocery cart or his wife who also is my aunt, and three kids. Roy walked once around the wreck, made The Cross, followed Paco to our rig. For sure now, all systems go.

I looked down my rows, but I see nothing: not married, have no U.S. papers.

I walked the other way, to the fence.

Paco is also my uncle, so no sweat. And he don't know for eighty-seven missions Mr. Sparger went north in Nam, get some gooks, or Sams. *Hey! That airplane eat your lunch.*

Also Mr. Sparger said, "Some future time we go up, take a hop. Okay?"

I said, "Mr. Sparger, allll right!"

Now Blue-Leader One is Mayday, MIA, out of it.

But even two fields away, always I saw the sun come out his spray nozzles.

Always I say only to me: Oh, you Blue-Leader One, Pull up, pull up!

Dump, dump! Return to Base, do you read me?

When I went over the fence Luis Martinis climbed in to take my place. Luis always waits at the fence, ready to go; Luis is not so fast, so he is not on regular.

A Toyota pickup gave me a ride to town.

I got off at the light, at the Mir-a-Mar.

This time not at the counter, but in a clean booth, I ordered for myself the best: the steak, the fries, the coffee now.

In the Mir-a-Mar, in my booth, the air was cool, and yet only two hours ago, I saw him come down my row, on the deck, the sun blazing his canopy under wires.

Now, on a television above their cash register I see *All the News at Noon.*

I left my booth, went to their television.

KJJX's cameraman is at the scene. This crash one mile south of 101 was fatal to veteran pilot of a single engine crop-duster based at Con-Agra's field only minutes from the crash site. Pilot's name being withheld pending notification of next-of-kin.

"Withheld," the Mir-a-Mar manager said, wiped his lips with a napkin. "Sparger got what was coming to him."

"Hey, no pilot error!"

Just then, on the television screen, I saw myself.

I was at the lower left, beside the crash. I was the dumb guy staring, holding a helmet by its strap. I was ashamed to be in that picture, his helmet in one hand, a piece of metal in the other.

The manager saw my picture on the screen, and said, "For sure you saw it?"

He liked that, and for one moment I felt famous on TV.

So I told everything to the manager.

"Low, right *above* your head? Well, Sparger was an asshole. And he could have killed you."

I told him Mr. Sparger's side. The mist. The sun.

"So okay, but he was two whole fields off. Dispatched to the Rossi plat, but went in on Halliday Farms. Besides he was a drunk. Every night here in the bar, bullshitting the general public. About Viet Nam."

The manager motioned towards their bar, in back.

On the sidewalk outside a big woman in a red kind of evening dress stopped, pressed her face against the Mir-a-Mar window. She was looking inside, but at noon no one was at the bar.

"Speaking of which," and the manager nodded towards the window, but the woman had walked on.

"Speaking of which, there's the second Mrs. Sparger-to-be. Six months now Sparger has his love nest with that baby. I didn't like to see them come in. Two of a kind."

I said nothing.

"I bet Number Two just heard the big news on TV. Now she's headed for Church. Both Catholic."

I went back to my booth.

This one time I had ordered the best, but now it was cold.

Afterwards, I was going on to the Church to light one candle, but his Number Two-to-be would do that. And so I never did.

The Rock Pool

The girl's sports car was a dust-covered animal running between the trees of the lane and then into their ranch yard.

From behind the screen of the kitchen door, Mr. Emerson watched her car skid and stop. Only then did the girl seem to realize the highway and the lane had come to an end so she turned off everything very quickly: her radio, the tape deck, the engine. As though it had caught up with her at last, a cloud of dust hunched above the car's hood, settled, and disappeared into the ranch-yard clay.

Even after it was all over and largely forgotten by the neighbors, Mr. Emerson remembered for some years the day the girl first parked so abruptly: her unnaturally blonde hair in contrast to the car's leatherette upholstery, the car itself a low daub of red against the upright, grey side of the barn; how the girl allowed her shoulders to slump for a moment, as though to turn herself off, as though she was never going to drive any place again.

She had seen his wife's Cabin-for-Rent sign three-quarters of a mile back towards the blacktop county road.

"I would," Mrs. Emerson told the girl after they had walked through the cattle gate and had walked side by side down the arroyo to see it.

The cabin was very nice: one room only, a refrigerator beside a pre-fab shower stall; a kitchenette, all very nicely furnished, of course; a double bed, bookshelves built right into the walls, and nice closets for blankets—surely not needed in this weather—and also extra pillowcases and sheets. From the steps of the porch one nice view was up towards the farm gate, the big ranch house, the Petrolane tank and the water pump enclosure screened by ferns; then another nice view was down to the foot of the rock steps which led to the pool—a wide, bulldozed place, walled with stones, and fed by water diverted from the creek. As for neighbors, nothing except ferns and the valley, a receding terrace of redwood trees all the way to Santa Cruz.

"Would have to collect also a last-month's rent, in advance," and because to this girl the austere, shed-roofed cabin above the rock pool was a place of immediate, windless peace, she counted out ten-dollar bills and did not inquire about utilities, or a rent receipt, or guests, or who would wash the sheets when the time came.

And no: the girl would require no help from Mr. Emerson to unload the car; and no, would not accept a warm first-meal in the Emerson ranch house because in the car there were leftover things to eat in a cardboard box.

Therefore the Emersons understood privacy was wanted, and complete independence from everything and everybody was the basic idea; and finally, no, there would be no real incoming mail, from any place, although it was nice to know the number of this Rural Route out of Santa Cruz.

While the Emersons ate strawberries from their own garden, they heard the first music from her car's tape deck, now transferred and hooked up inside the cabin, playing through her portable radio, playing very loud, very electronic guitar music.

At eleven, when Mr. and Mrs. Emerson were side by side, not touching or even thinking of anything like that, the girl's cassettes turned out the identical chords again and again. The sounds overflowed the cabin and filled the rock pool and the whole arroyo.

"From San Francisco, heading south?"

"Judging from the dust, perhaps from New Mexico, by way of Bakersfield. Headed north."

"Or an airline stewardess?"

"I'm Sadie," Mr. Emerson said, "fly me to Miami." And Mrs. Emerson said, "Huh!"

After a minute Mrs. Emerson said, "Well, I will visit her," for in most cases the Truth would come out.

Mr. Emerson almost said, "I'll take a look myself," but the implication was not good.

This month he was fifty-nine years old and the wife was pretty much past doing much along *those* lines. He accepted it: now she pretty much dug in her own flower beds—and that was that.

Nevertheless, Mr. Emerson remembered precisely the inflamed, greedy moment he had offered to carry the girl's expensive suitcase into the cabin. Beside the opened trunk of her car he had sensed her fragility, her brittleness, and also a kind of desperation which was vulnerable and also inviting.

In a voice calculated to suggest this day was almost over, Mr. Emerson said, "I'll check her registration slip sometime. In the car."

"Well, that young lady came from *some*place . . ."

Abruptly, because their own front door might not be

locked, Mr. Emerson got up. He walked through the familiar rooms to the side windows. Just then the lights of the cabin switched off; the music abruptly stopped. Through the windowpane he saw the straight edge of the cabin roof against a third-quarter moon above the arroyo. And wouldn't the girl be in the double bed, beneath clean sheets, with possibly nothing on at all, or however she slept?

After Mr. Emerson returned to their own queen-sized, childless bed he suppressed everything he had felt or had thought. Partly to avoid thinking at all about the girl and partly to divert any possible suspicions he said, "You were a smart woman. To work it out. Never honestly thought you would rent it. Away out here."

"There is always someone," Mrs. Emerson said, and again she felt justified, complete. The month-in-advance was also money in the bank no matter what might happen.

Mrs. Emerson turned once and gave herself to the marble landscapes of all sleep.

II

For ten days the girl lived alone in the rental cabin. Each morning and each afternoon on a ledge of rock she felt she healed herself by dozing in the sun or by staring at creek debris which by chance entered the pool, circled twice with the current, and then floated downstream over boulders.

Later, when they talked about the exact moment it began, the girl said she was not even surprised when higher up along a path the first two rocks dislodged and bounced down, and then she heard footsteps coming.

When the girl looked up, the man—a boy really—came out of the brush to the pool's edge. She knew at once he was hiking for he had a backpack of blue and a matching canteen.

Later, when they talked about the exact moment it began, the boy recalled he had first seen the white Petrolane tank humped in ferns, and the cabin roof against the sky, and then—while looking across the pool for a path that might take him to a road—only then did he see the girl sunbathing on a shelf of rock.

What he wanted most was to fill the blue canteen, and of course the pool looked very pure but then pollutants were everywhere . . .

She felt the boy was probably three years younger—so would be just out of high school. And as it turned out, to celebrate graduation, his parents had sponsored this cross-country hike, a different, really outdoor way to see the West. That's why he was hiking south: had entered the woods just below San Francisco and had followed the earth's contours with a very detailed surveyor's map. When he traced the route until now, she saw he really had come in a beeline, and eventually would touch the coast just north of Monterey Bay.

David followed her along the cut-out stone steps to the cabin. There she ran water from the tap until they heard the pump of the engine begin to work in the ferns beside the Petrolane tank. When the water was cold he drank a very great deal and then he sat down on the floor, his pack propped against the white stall of the shower.

Looking back on it a week later, they agreed it was almost exactly in this way that their relationship began.

III

After supper the Emersons sat on their front porch to watch the pelt-like shadows of evening take first the redwoods, and then the upper meadow, and finally the long valley towards Santa Cruz and the sea.

"That boy is somewhat younger," Mrs. Emerson said. On the pretense of delivering the rent receipt and also a calculated, above-criticism loaf of warm nut-and-raisin bread, she had visited the little house. At noon she saw the young man in blue bathing trunks stretched out big as life on the opposite side of the pool. "Also of some background and manners, if standing up for introduction to an older woman signifies . . ."

David was the first name. And in the present fashion, last name not stated.

Even in the darkness of their porch, however, Mrs. Emerson did not disclose her first, uncalculated reaction; for some years she had well understood how tolerant J. W. could be regarding the so-called private conduct of others. Yet she knew her first reaction was a fact and when she saw the two, separate, distinct growths of white flesh on the rock ledge above the water, she thought: what about later?

And yet, instantly, that feeling gave way to a resentment. She knew her resentment was also a fact. She hated the casualness of it, the way they were lying not very far apart in the reverberating heat of the arroyo walls, with nothing better to do with themselves when she, herself, had been up since daylight, had already done a full day's work.

Actually, Mrs. Emerson had paused beside the cabin porch to make certain it was not her imagination and then she called "Yoo-hoo" towards the blonde young thing stretched out like a half-naked lizard on a rock, and then walked down the steps to deliver receipt and bread pan—and very naturally getting a closer look at them both.

"Thanks," the young woman said, and tucked the rent receipt between the bread loaf and the pan.

"This is David," and the young man smiled and put out his hand.

If no last name revealed, probably this visit was temporary, so as yet no real chance to give the cabin a bad name.

There was a bird-whistle-and-wind kind of silence. Because the boy was a little shy, and because the young woman seemed never to say anything at all, Mrs. Emerson said very cheerily, "See you two. Later."

As she turned, the young man called after her and she came back.

"Is it okay?" and David spoke very openly, very innocently. "If I rest here. Awhile?"

If the young woman felt anything at all, if she had prior knowledge of the question, if she actually heard the question, she gave no sign, no hint of any future involvement. The boy was asking this simply for himself.

"Why yes," Mrs. Emerson had to say with a hearty, country hospitality. And then when she saw other implications, she denied even partial responsibility for anything that might come to pass. "That's entirely up—to—ah—to *her*."

Again the young woman neither replied nor changed expression, and so with a country woman's accommodation of both neighborliness and a kind of outrage almost entirely suppressed, Mrs. Emerson turned up the stairs again and said back over her shoulder, "So long, you two."

Once through the ranch-yard gate, and out of sight, Mrs. Emerson changed dresses quickly. Then she went into the side yard and weeded and deep-hoed a flower bed which was not at all doing well for July.

Now, on the front porch, they could not see each other's face.

In silence they rocked, as was their habit. Towards bedtime Mr. Emerson recalled once more with absolute clarity what he, himself, had seen past noon.

Actually he had spent the morning with the back-pasture well. Then, upon return to the barn, he thought, Why not take a look at the rental cabin pump? So, since his hands were already greasy, he went there and that's why he had the toolbox open and the cover off the pump when the girl came out of the cabin.

The girl's buttocks were really mature and there was in her walk a movement, a thing which signaled loose-ness, at the right time doing—well, doing everything . . .

Halfway down the carved-out steps of stone, the girl finished tying her straps. From above, through ferns, Mr. Emerson saw the bed-sheet white of her breast—actually only half a breast. But he saw it. Just like that.

What he felt and what he wanted to feel was pure, and lustful, and entirely bestial, the way he always felt when he watched animals on the farm do the job—and then absolutely forget what had just happened to them. It was a feeling he knew and a feeling he never denied to himself.

Deliberately, Mr. Emerson came back to business, to the pump. He placed one hand on the electric motor housing—warm; he touched the drive belt—good ten-sion; the fifty-gallon tank—full. Only a drop of oil was needed, and also a half-turn of the grease cup on the main shaft . . .

When he looked down again through the parapet of

ferns, the girl was sunning. Her hair lay windblown across the rock; her shoulders were no match at all for stone outcrop. Her legs were together—just now—but at the right time the position of the legs could be changed, could be spread out . . .

For some little time Mr. Emerson looked down through ferns to the pool below. Wrench in hand, immobile, without present or even any future hope of direct satisfaction, he permitted his desire to float upward like water rising in the rock pool, from his genitals to his lungs and to his head. All of this he felt was given to him on his own property. So he watched deliberately, for such was his privilege.

Just then he thought of Betsy, of Mrs. Emerson, in one of her characteristic positions: flower bed, weeding, pulling out roots and soil and hitting the root ends on the back of a shovel. For one moment the vision of Betsy, of Mrs. Emerson, and the younger woman stretched out beside the pool merged and blurred contrapuntally in his mind.

Below, the cabin door slammed.

The young man also walked from the cabin porch and down the stone steps. He was slender and young, his head watching his own feet carefully as he walked across hot shale. As Mr. Emerson watched, the younger man found his own ledge of stone, somewhat larger and immediately below the girl. Of this he was absolutely certain: the pair of them were on the same side of the pool, closer together than in the morning, or even at noon.

On their porch, in the dark, Mr. Emerson stopped rocking.

"On a cross-country hike, you said? Out here from Ohio to see some real country? Well, he came to the right place, it's all right here," and although his speech was benign, was totally conversational, he thought of what must surely happen when the pair of them went back up the steps and into the cabin to get something to eat: wouldn't they have to change clothes in the single room? Why, there was no privacy at all, in just one single room.

"No harm in it," he added very easily for he understood Betsy was about to say, "What are you going to do about it, J. W.?"

Things between them went that way: in the first instance the cabin was her idea; therefore the rent money was hers to spend just any old way. Yet if something came up which had implications beyond the property lines of the ranch, something which might bring discredit on their home, then Betsy referred such matters to him.

"Why it's her privilege," Mr. Emerson said forthrightly, and saw no reason to interfere.

"Yes," and Mrs. Emerson saw J. W. was entirely right as she, herself, had said as much this morning. "She can have two dozen guests—for all we care."

They went to bed.

Without consciously wanting to do so, Mrs. Emerson discouraged his hand on her thigh, much less on her breast. Having a new girl around the place would make a difference no doubt, and yet she said, "I weeded *all* day—and the side-bed does look better . . ."

Mr. Emerson heard the implication of her voice—and that was that.

Nevertheless, as was his privilege, Mr. Emerson recalled deliberately the sunlight on the vivid disorder of blonde hair athwart an outcrop of shale. Then he caused himself to imagine the girl lying on the rock—like that—with no clothes on at all.

After one minute of abstract yet almost total satisfaction, without either guilt or remorse, he came back to his own responsibilities, and to what might be done if things got out of hand. "I'll get a look at her car registration. Sometime this week."

By then Mrs. Emerson was in the first shallow tidepools of sleep, dreaming nothing at all.

IV

For more than ten nights, the boy slept on his blue, duck-down bag. When the sun came above the upper tier of redwoods each morning, he turned his face to the wall; in the large double bed across the room he heard Sands also change her position in order to avoid the light and in this way to sleep each day until ten o'clock.

Although it was his habit to rise early, the boy now took his daily patterns from Sands, and in this way he could think about everything: was there a larger pattern in that he had found this cabin only a few days after—by entirely different means—after Sands had also discovered it?

As to Sands, herself, it was still a puzzle. She seldom spoke. Mostly she worked by gestures of the head, of the hand. He wanted to know more, but he felt the last thing permitted him, as a guest, was to make direct inquiry.

So: if her name was Sands, was this after the novelist, or was it a family name? If she had left someplace very quickly, was she in flight from school, or family, or—perhaps—a boyfriend? Because she was so awkward in the kitchenette and could not make up a bed, had she ever worked, anywhere?

So: from her luggage tags and from a discarded envelope, she was connected with the Summer School at Arizona State University. Also about the Triumph automobile, Sands said ironically, "Why *his*. Wouldn't you *know* it?" Namely, her brother's car. She kept the car parked as much as possible. Why?

Beyond these few things, he understood Sands was thinking, allowing the sun to bake from mind and body the things she had abandoned, or fled, and which might still pursue her. Mostly because of an undefined pity, the boy made himself sensitive to her mood. Therefore, he also used only a few words each day—and that was enough.

Finally, the boy felt he had earned the right to hold up the last used and reused tea bag, and to laugh with her, and to say, "Sands, toss me the car keys?"

He drove back from Santa Cruz with many cardboard boxes.

Together, laughing a great deal because Sands really did like everything he brought back to the cabin, they stored the food on the shelves or in the refrigerator: one dozen assorted TV dinners; packettes of Snax, pretzels, crackers, potato chips, E-Z Thins, and five water-tumbler deals of processed cheese, including a phoney Gorgonzola. Then Cola and Orange and Root Beer and two bottles of Cold Duck—all good stuff. In the last four boxes were the canned goods, the gut things to keep them eating well for quite a long time: smoked oysters, sardines, canned soups, canned crab, and finally many packages of hot dogs, real buns, totally organic honey, and new-baked bread, 94 percent wheat germ. Finally, he showed her the two top-twenty, long-play cassettes by the Leadfoot Family Four—*right* on.

After the initial food-run to Santa Cruz, the boy prepared all the food; he understood that unless someone took charge Sands only snacked and nibbled late at night while they listened again and again to the new cassettes. Cautiously, he changed certain of their life patterns, but nevertheless each day they sunned on the rocks and talked about Mysticism and Faith; the Games Aspect of Life; and what happened, if anything, after so-called death. He was exactly three years younger, had gone to a private school, and had read a great deal; she seemed considerably older, said nothing at all about any high school, and tempered what he said by her "experience." By night, because it was softer, they now lay side by side on the double bed. When he turned off their light they listened, together, to the sounds of the night and the water filling the rock pool and to the water going away across boulders and down to the valley and to the sea beyond.

Several times they said it to each other: their relationship was very much like being brother and sister.

As the days passed they talked more and more about everything. Now they lay on the rocks with no clothes on at all because Sands wanted a perfect tan, with no strap marks showing. Finally they talked directly about sex, the thing he most wanted to discuss, but which until now, with every person he had ever known, had always eluded him.

"No," and the boy felt in all honesty she should know this final, unnatural, thwarted thing about him. "Not ever. With anyone."

Neither of them spoke. The sun overhead beat the surface of the pool like a drum.

In his own shameful confession he heard the real reason he had left home for the summer and had elaborately disguised his intention as a "wilderness opportunity": in fact, he had left home to seek something unknown and what he had found was a cabin among redwoods and a rock pool below.

In his voice she heard the irresolution, the shame, and the terrible lack of confidence in himself; all those things combined to form a desperate necessity for assertion not yet clearly understood even by himself. More than anything she wanted to say what he needed to hear, with no thought of the future.

"Oh, men mature much *later* than girls," she said and as she placed her hand on his arm for the first time she touched his flesh and felt a secret, tender satisfaction which always before had been kept from her. Then in order to experience this new feeling once more, she said, "Especially in a *boys* school. You just had no opportunity, you see?"

"Right," he said, and he saw this was his exact case. Partly because he spoke to her outspread hair, he tried to be honest about it. "No opportunity—ah, that was *meaningful.*"

"But *you* have?" he asked directly for he wanted terribly to know this one very important, secret thing about her past.

"Oh all girls have to get around," and she said this not so much to his averted face as to the shelf of rock where they were sunning with no clothes on at all.

"That's what our English teacher pointed out about Milton: there is no such thing as cloistered virtue."

Those words meant nothing at all to her, but everything instantly came back to her, and it was as though the creek had suddenly risen, had overflowed its banks, had overwhelmed and washed away even the cabin.

From the beginning she felt she had planned it so: the night of her fourteenth birthday party, with Ray, at his house, in his own room because . . . Then for a long time with Ken who was much more of a leader. Then the next year, in August, at the so-called Church Camp, it was a way to know everybody better, to be outstanding because . . . And then in high school, in Tucson, it was . . . and she braced her shoulders against the stone outcrop, as though all of the memories of the group in Tucson would go away.

By then even her own brother knew where she went every afternoon at three o'clock, and came home promptly at half-past five when her father always said, "Well, what did you learn today?"

Math, he always said, was very important.

The officers in plain clothes visited the high school. They searched lockers. They found what they thought was a lot of stuff. Then it was "confidential" interviews which only the PTA, the sheriff's office, and the high-school newspaper editor knew about. Before Christmas her older sister, who always knew it all, came back from Bennington "to help." Even her father, who now thought some things were even more important than math, did not suggest she attend college. The idea was to "reach maturity," and never to see the old high-school crowd ever again, except . . . So she spent more than a year at home, in her own room, and nothing happened.

Later friends of her mother got her admitted to an "experimental" Summer Session in California: success there indicated real college in the fall. The family psychiatrist very much agreed: get away from home; get away from Tucson. That was the first step. But a step towards what?

In fact it was a step towards cashing the Summer Session check for tuition and fees; a step towards the bus which finally took her to Newport Beach to see her brother—where the car was. Her brother was nice but this time he said if she ever took his sports car again, they were really through.

So she drove his car away at two o'clock in the morning, drove north, and before noon turned off the freeway to avoid the Highway Patrol, and finally when she was ready to scream because of the sun, she had seen the Cabin-for-Rent sign beside the Emersons' mailbox. For sure, her tuition check had cleared her father's bank account.

All these things she kept to herself, for after the first ten days in this out-of-the-way, secret place she understood absolutely that everything was a matter of coming to terms, of acceptance of herself. Partly because David arrived, partly because they had talked about so many things, but mostly because she had understood it was only herself whom she tore into pieces, she had made up her mind: in two days she would call her brother in Newport Beach to tell him the exact date she would return his car and also exactly how many miles were now registered on the odometer.

David was talking to her.

"For you, Sands," and he wanted very much to hear her confirm it, "it was—well, meaningful? Always?"

"Yes," she said, and she felt it was the only lie in her whole life she would ever tell him.

Although her eyes were closed against all of the past and against the drum beats of the overhead sun, she felt his hand for the first time stroking her shattered, outspread hair.

In a moment, abruptly, the boy stood up.

He had felt the first breeze of late afternoon. Therefore to protect her he went back to the cabin to put something on and to bring back an orange drink and her robe.

From the porch of the cabin, farther up the hill among ferns, he saw Mr. Emerson again repairing their water pump.

Late that night after the cassettes played again and again, after he had turned off the light, when everything outside except the creek was silent, the girl stood in the moonlight beside the bed. She reached down and took the boy's hand. When he was standing beside her, in a fine, new way, she pressed her body close to his. For the first time she felt his lips on her flesh—first only on her neck . . .

That night the girl began to teach him everything that she knew, but only a little at a time. Like giving lessons. Yes, like giving useful, necessary lessons to someone not at all a stranger, and yet not precisely a younger brother, but above all to someone who was no threat, and who was hers, from the beginning alone.

V

"I cannot and I will not," Mrs. Emerson stated to J. W. from her side of their bed. "Cannot condone what they are now doing in broad daylight; will not condone the wrong and the sinful which might well bring a plaintiff suit and resultant scandal countywide . . ."

Over the years Mr. Emerson had learned to wait. Often Betsy went on like this. In the end, nearly always, she listened to reason.

"Also, to judge by their garbage can, if it isn't paper or tinfoil, then it isn't food—and all our nice fruit in season . . ." She rolled once beneath the sheets. The totally brittle nature of all those TV dinners, the boy's furtive food-runs to Santa Cruz, the identical music playing again and again until all hours, the total modernity of it offended. Taken together their days and their nights seemed so wasteful, so improvident.

From his side of their bed, Mr. Emerson did not confide his opinion. Besides repairing the cabin water pump more than once, he now knew even better places which looked right down into the cabin. Also on no particular schedule he carried away their trash; also he delivered letters from the boy's parents in Ohio. Putting everything together, he saw only two young people—lucky ones—who would probably stay on until Labor Day and then the whole thing would end naturally enough. If the girl was somewhat older, he was well pleased to observe she was not now quite so withdrawn, so silent. When she ran up the steps to get more letters from Ohio, she always said, "Many happy returns," and laughed, and threw back her hair, and then ran away to find the young man who was off someplace looking for new paths. Once he delivered the mail right to the door, and she was just getting into her robe. What was happening was maybe good for everyone.

"Out," Mrs. Emerson said. "Out *she* goes."

"No real harm in it," he said very firmly, and of course it was true: he imagined himself reared above that young woman, doing what was necessary, and yet at the same time accepting the fact that it was only an older man's notion, and not at all possible for him—and it never had been, in all his life. Yet he wanted to prolong their stay, for the benefit of all concerned. "You already have her money."

Because he had added nothing to the case, Mrs. Emerson said nothing at all.

Partly to cover his own tracks, and partly to delay any possible trouble ahead, Mr. Emerson added, "I got a look at the registration. I jotted it down. Probably her brother's car. From Newport Beach."

"That's good," Mrs. Emerson said in a forgiving, conciliatory way, and ended it for tonight. An address and a two-dollar telephone call, and possibly a referral to the young woman's mother—if she had one—those things were now possible. It was a strength to know a name was written down on the back of an envelope, a little bit like having money in the bank.

And yet resentment was what she felt. Mr. J. W. Emerson was just a little too interested, had repaired the cabin pump once too often. If not personally interested in the spectacle, why not save time for all concerned by delivering their mail *and* at the same time collect their garbage?

She thought of herself, on hands and knees, weeding a flower bed. She thought of J. W.—no shirt on at all— sunning on a rock, lying between the two of them, lying between that David and that maybe out-of-work airline stewardess old enough to know better.

Even though she knew these images were neither true nor remotely possible, Mrs. Emerson lay awake for a long time listening again and again to the cabin's music.

VI

Two days after the operator put through Mrs. Emerson's telephone call to Arizona, the girl's mother arrived: first by air from the Great Southwest; then by rented car from the San Jose airport, direct. Mrs. Emerson's telephone directions were accurate, and it was no trouble at all to find the county road, and the mailbox, and the lane.

First the mother accepted the kind invitation of Mr. Emerson to step into the living room for a little chat. Without it being said in so many words, Mrs. Emerson understood there had been trouble before—and not surprisingly if what we read in the newspapers is even half true. Apparently there had been "professional help" in the not-distant past; and surely this second daughter had grown up between two over-achievers. Not good. Behind that, there was the City of Tucson, itself. And behind that . . .

Mr. Emerson managed to disappear from the living room before Mrs. Emerson took the girl's mother to the gate and pointed out the roof of the cabin and the rock pool below.

"Why, I'd know it anywhere!" the girl's mother said in an indignant, suppressed way. "Why, that's Herbert's T-4."

Because Mr. Emerson got to the cabin first, the boy and the girl were now already up and dressed.

The boy wore hiking boots. The bed roll and a canteen full of water were already strapped in place.

The rest of it was no business of hers, so Mrs. Emerson turned back from the gate and walked to the house to wash the coffee service.

Mr. Emerson, however, checked the gauge on the Petrolane tank, and that way looked down on the three of them: the boy, with the pack on his back; the girl, for the first time wearing red slacks; the mother. Together they stood on the cabin porch, talking very politely for almost five minutes.

Before the mother and the girl went inside the cabin together, the boy shook hands and then without turning to wave he went around the edge of the pool and on down a path to the lower stand of redwoods. By nightfall he would be in Santa Cruz where he had wanted to go in the first place.

When there was no one left on the porch at all, Mr. Emerson stood motionless in the ferns for a long moment. Then he decided he might as well get at it: there was still enough time left of this morning to repair some fence.

VII

Later, in mid-October, at about two-thirty in the morning, Mr. Emerson awoke: he heard an automobile stop in the ranch yard—no lights. He heard the gate above the arroyo open. He heard the automobile coast forward over gravel. The gate closed.

Without having to get up or even put on his shoes or go out beneath an overcast October sky to make certain, he knew the girl had returned. Wouldn't she have hidden a key, or have kept a key from the time she rented during the summer?

What he felt was a sudden excitement—and a terrible pity. Without willing it so, he remembered her blonde hair scattered in the desperate sunshine and her evenly tanned flesh—and no strap marks. For a moment, he thought she had come back because of himself. But no.

Nevertheless, in that memory of her, he recognized all of the wasted—yet productive—years of his life. For a few weeks she had revived in him the failed passion of all their married life. Oh, he watched all right, but mostly because he had grown up in a different era, when to look was the only thing most men were able to do. But no, it could never work out. What he wanted was for the girl to stay in the cabin—either alone or with somebody—for a very long time.

Until daylight, there was nothing for it except to lie awake, his back rigid against the stone ledge of their mattress. After breakfast, casually, he might walk down to the cabin to see if it was an automobile, after all.

Later he told the sheriff. After that he told the coroner's people. He told them exactly what he had seen and had thought. He started with the moment he first opened the gate:

Unbeknownst to either Betsy or himself, probably during the morning hours, this small Chevy sedan had parked beside their little rental place.

That seemed strange. Therefore he checked the locks on the cabin: no sign of entry, illegal or otherwise.

When he turned from the cabin door, why naturally he looked down the steps and into the rock pool. That's when he saw the body. Half-afloat it was and very steadily turning around and around with the current. Quickly he ran down the steps because it had to be the same one who rented during the summer. It had to be the same one because even from above, on the steps, her blonde hair floated in an odd, spread-out way.

If there were needle marks or any kind of puncture marks any place on the girl's body, the coroner kept it out of the autopsy.

As for the boy, David, he was easy enough to check: he answered the telephone himself and had been all week in his dormitory at Oberlin College. The sheriff did not disclose the nature of the case, but said only that this was a routine call.

"A terrible thing for the girl's parents," Mrs. Emerson later told the interested neighbors. "Both parents professional people, the mother with a masters in Economics. Also a tragedy for Tucson and to all those who knew her."

Privately, however, Mrs. Emerson surmised the girl came back to do what she had intended to do in the first place. But because the cabin was so nicely situated—with its view of the creek, and the valley beyond—and everything inside so nicely furnished, why no doubt that helped delay the girl's plan—for a time. And then Mrs. Emerson always added, "Of course, when she came back that second time, she was not really our tenant anymore."

When Mr. Emerson heard Betsy say that, he understood it was her way of making certain the little rental cabin did not get a bad name.

How Old Man Found What Was Lost

That time was in Ohio long ago when people lived on farms and did the work themselves but had electric lights inside the rooms and a radio to get the News and tractors and many well-known animals such as cows. Also many dogs in the farm yard all barking and running around in circles.

Farmer and Old Woman lived and worked on just such a farm: for many a year it was corn, hogs, wheat, and soybeans or maybe clover. Once they had children about the house but not any more as three daughters, each in turn, went off to live a better life in Cincinnati.

One August about midnight Farmer stood on his front porch and looked out across his one hundred six-four acres of corn and heard the corn growing, making springy little noises in the dark clear back to his woods. Farmer looked once at the sky and then he locked all outside doors, but did not go very fast upstairs to where their bed was.

First, as was customary, Farmer turned off the electric light and then took off all his clothes and then laid hisself down beside Old Woman.

–Hotter, Farmer said, than a half-fixed fox in a forest fire.

Even when he didn't know it, Old Woman understood everything about Farmer; therefore his remark told Old Woman what was on Farmer's mind—maybe.

As that thought was some real change in things, Old Woman decided to find out the lay of the land.

Old Woman half-rolled over to Farmer's side and she placed her leg almost on top of his leg. Old Woman felt she had the rights of it because Farmer hisself first mentioned fox.

Very softly Old Woman said into the pillow beside Farmer's ear, "Hooo?"

In times past when Farmer was young or had just returned from the stockyards with money or of an afternoon had walked through his barns to view breeding stock or if the corn was well along, then he nearit always said,

–Hooo, yourself . . . ? and then in various ways the job got done, and that was that.

In the past there had been some real Hoooing around. But lately not much, which is what is being said.

As was natural, Old Woman understood Farmer was getting on in years. Moreover, the three girls were not longer about the house, taxes were up some, the neighbors talked drought, drought, and of recent date a blood virus taken down two shoats per week all of which signified losses for everybody.

Well, this very day, Old Woman, herself, had done no work—except a little fancy tatting. She skipped the News and went direct upstairs full well knowing Farmer was soon to follow as he did not much like to be alone in the rooms of their house. Old Woman had something on *her* mind.

–I pass, Farmer said, and for the first time in his life felt bad to renege—the corn being so well along. To renege made him feel unnaturally old. Farmer had well noted Old Woman tatting fast all afternoon, so knowed he was in for it.

Old Woman did not say anything at once for she understood his remark might be natural for a man of his years, though otherwise healthy and of good appetite.

Nevertheless, three months of I Pass was a considerable time. So Old Woman retch over and with her hand slid down the nice black hair of Farmer's belly. With her hand sometimes, as in play, she would find it and then take aholt of his business.

This time no business. Nothing—so to speak—for Old Woman to take aholt of.

–That's why I passed, Farmer said, and he was put out to let her know something. Seems I lost it. Lost . . . my business.

Again Old Woman said nothing. But since she knew all of that territory very well, had looked it over many a time in broad daylight, she just very gentle, gentle searched around. Just looking for herself with her woman hand.

Old Woman was also some surprised. As Farmer claimed, there was not much in fact nothing in the whole territory.

Then Old Woman whispered very kindly in his ear, "Well, let's just see about this," and before Farmer could say I, Yes, No nor Flour, why out their bed she sprang and turned on the electric light and—bang—she pulled back their coverlet.

And that was that.

For Old Woman to see him like that was always a sight: good legs and arms, and those shoulders, and his face maybe a little creased from the work and the sun as though afloat on the clean sheets, and ifn he opened those eyes they was blue as an ocean . . .

Very closely, she inspected the whole territory, a thing which even under the circumstances gave some trifle of pleasure . . . Then she turned out the light, got back in bed, and caused herself to lie down next to Farmer. Hooo, she said, it's some little thing. Besides, Hog Futures are steady, the girls are happy in Cincinnati, and your corn is well along. Tomorrow I'll kill us a chicken, largely for the dumplins . . .

In his mind, Farmer saw what she said in clear pictures. There was much to be thankful for so after the chicken wouldn't they just rock on the porch and listen to the corn grow?

Old Woman went to sleep and then Farmer went to sleep—called it a day.

Well no change in the Hoooing, but Old Woman saw Farmer look everywhere: looked in the little toolbox under the seat of the wheat binder; among sacks of clover seed because of the sweet, attracting smell; looked under the Leghorn hen because of her steady warmth—but nowhere around the place was his business to be found.

Not found, not mentioned, was Old Woman's thought and besides, twixt her and the gate post, she understood nothing was really lost: gradually it had become smaller and smaller, and now it was back where it came from. So at this moment it was at hand, in Farmer's belly. So to Old Woman it boilt down to this: salt the cow to get the calf, for she knew of old that it was never out never up.

In her ways, Old Woman was very smart, so the morning after Labor Day, as was her plan all along, she lay abed. No reason stated.

Come noon, Farmer went to the bedroom to see about it, there being no dinner cooked.

Still Old Woman faced the wall: taken her bed.

Four days passed and no meals forthcoming, so towards noon Farmer was back again to the bedroom and in effect said, We ought to Doctor. We ought to Doctor some.

"No Doctoring," Old Woman said very bravely. "It's too much money."

Which was a point.

Four more days passed, and no change. Mostly to get things organized, and also because Old Woman could be stubborn as the off-mule in a sorghum mill, in effect Farmer said, You will have it, so I'll fetch the Bailey girl from town. She can look to your needs, and cook some, and how much all-found a week oughten I offer her mother?

"Whatever is right," Old Woman said, and faced the wall.

So next day, back from town, up pulls Farmer in his automobile, and he parks her in the center of the barn-yard.

Farmer gets out. He walks him around the radiator, and he opens *her* door. Out steps this Bailey girl: all found, and wearing a starched, all-white uniform borrowed of her mother (also betimes a practical nurse).

Then all Billy-bedamned braked loose in that barn-yard: dogs barking and running in circles; the yellow she-cat and half her litter a-streaked for the crib; Jim-the-Crow calling *Hey-Petey, Hey-Petey* from the grape arbor; the two mules poked their heads out the hog-pen winders.

That Bailey girl were a lot better framed than most. Also a redhead. Also in the wind of the ruckus, holting down her dress hem with one hand: that Bailey girl's all-white uniform roilt up everything.

All of which signified not much in the bedroom, in private, when Old Woman laid out the work expected:

"Some light housekeeping," Old Woman said, and sat up real sprite on the edge of her bed. "But don't feed too heavy."

The Bailey girl took Old Woman's meaning: easy on the meat.

"And this next is betwixt just the two of us: though active, Farmer has got two failings. One, the left ear is not quite deef as a fence post. Second, his sight. Things close at hand he can not see too good—like hand tools, or a knife and fork. Naturally, Farmer has got his pride so never lets on. Even to me.

"That's why," Old Woman continued, "Farmer is your real patient. But pretend it's me. Stay plenty outside with him, and from time-to-time I'll get my own tea water."

The Bailey girl took Old Woman's meaning: speak up to the left ear; help find little things at hand; keep a shut mouth, especially to Farmer.

"All correct," said Old Woman, and began to straighten up her bed.

Meanwhile Farmer was gone to the barn to see why two mules poked their heads out of two winders of a brood sow's pen.

Inside bright and early for two weeks it was a red-head and a white uniform in the kitchen. It was Here's your aigs—no bacon, it's too dear; it was Here's your coffee and your knife, and she took Farmer's hand and gentle found him his fork.

"Also," says the Bailey girl, and because Farmer flinched some she knew his hearing was now some better so she whispered real close, "And here's your napkun."

"Yes sir," Farmer said, and he thought, Napkun for breakfast?

For two weeks outside it was the Bailey girl helping Farmer, her white uniform now normal, the stock not roilt up.

Farmer was looking for something, like a blind dog in a meat house. Naturally, Farmer couldn't exactly describe it to a stranger, so the Bailey girl did her best, fetched him bolts, a lynch pin, a staple puller, a clevis, and held them close to Farmer's nose and said, "Is this it?"

Course it never was.

Gradual, however, Farmer gave it up, and only slicked down some harness, greased all wagon axles, and cleaned some clover seed. But the Bailey girl was there, *handing* him every little thing, close, and sometimes more so.

Then Old Woman heard Farmer sing "Tenting Tonight" in the privy, and his laid-by corn never looked better. From her upstairs winder, Old Woman saw a white uniform always by Farmer's side. Well she noted Farmer was getting lively, and more so, which is what is being said.

So: the Bailey girl is in the corn crib. To get something dropped, she laid herself down and she retched down between some sacks of clover seed, stretched out cattywampus in her white uniform on the sacks.

Suddenly Farmer went outside to relieve hisself. And, well, there it was. Back in the same territory: he found his business.

Farmer came running back to the crib—to tell someone the news.

He saw the Bailey girl laid out on the clover sacks and Farmer just couldn't help hisself. He pinched her. Right there. On the uniform.

The Bailey girl come up off the clover sacks like a she-cat at weaning. She cuffed Farmer. On his good ear.

"If I want my ass pinched," she yelled, "I'll get it done in town and I quit."

So the Bailey girl packed her jockey box and Old Woman paid her off and Farmer drove her back to town no words spoke.

Back home Old Woman was hard at it: smoke in the kitchen, and a nice fryer in the pan.

"Good riddance," Old Woman said without hard feelings. "Hired help is never the same and she wasn't feeding you anyways near enough meats. And I knew it . . ."

Old Woman began to hum a song over the stove and everything was organized and back to normal.

That night in their bed, right away, Farmer said, "Hooo . . ." and Old Woman said, "Why Hooooo, yourself. . . ."

And the job got done. And for sometime there was plenty of Hoooing on the old home place in one way and another.

Though never so much as mentioning the Bailey girl again, the Old Woman thought this: it helped Farmer over a little drought, and she, herself, got some much-needed bed rest. So the expense was just about fifty-fifty, and it might be called Doctoring. Besides, they had never talked Florida vacation or anything like that.

What is general knowledge, howsomeever, is this: a few years later, whilst weeding an Iris bed, Old Woman just died. Soon thereafter Farmer died of a broken heart because he couldn't stand being alone in the rooms of their house.

Also general knowledge: the three daughters came home and naturally put the land, the stock, and all machinery to public auction. Jim-the-Crow went back to the woods; bids on livestock was stronger than expected.

The daughters settled their three shares with no

hard feelings and went their separate ways back to the City.

And that is how Farmer found what was temporary lost.

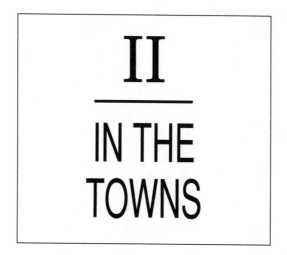

II

IN THE TOWNS

A Session of Summer

He said yes, and had so quickly inserted a key into the locked door of the building which once was the old University Gymnasium, and had so quickly walked inside and downstairs to the edge that she also noiselessly took off her clothes except for panties and dropped herself like a phantom into the tile, glimmering pool.

The water lapped at her nostrils—warmer than she had imagined.

These weeks of summer school had seared the lawns, had reduced the campus "river" to mud banks, but even after one second of thought she was surprised that a swimming pool in the basement of the old gym even at night could be so hot. She held her breath daintily, sidestroked towards a depth that would cover where her breasts were. He swam after her, following, very much like an eighth-grade math teacher. He paddled almost to her side, but did not yet touch her.

–Cools off, huh? he said in a whisper. His voice, however, was from habit and training very strident. His echoes went again over the tops of the wavelets, buried themselves finally in the sheer walls of tile.

–Well yes. It *does*, she admitted. Nor did it occur how easily he had been able to change their usual walk from the graduate stalls of the main library: on the way towards the bridge over the campus river he had revealed the towels folded very small in his briefcase. Before she could speak he had vectored her through what seemed a solid wall of the now-abandoned gymnasium.

Summer school was almost over. Examinations and their final papers on Education were due in one more week. He would take his master's degree; she would go back once more to the consolidated school at Pleasant Plain. By Labor Day the first teachers' meeting would be over and all the suntans that her friends had so painfully acquired would begin to fade. She knew he was married—he wore the ring—but because they had gossiped all this summer about university professors and had sat beside each other in classes, and because he had bought her soft drinks and had waited in the aisles of book stores, it seemed as though they really were only college students.

Besides they had in common their years in the consolidated high schools, being bullied by successful coaches and ambitious supervisors. They had known all the junior-senior banquets, the peas, the slice of ham, the pineapple ring, the bricks of melting ice cream with a class numeral in the center. They had been in opposite sections of the state, but they found the noisy hallways of their existence had driven them both to do those crazy things: at home he had lied about going to the movies; instead, he had become a regular at the "Golf Club" at the other end of town; all the negro musicians knew him; though she did not admit it, during the winter she sometimes slept in black lace gowns astride a pillow.

So, outside the old gymnasium when he said, I got a
pool in there, she had been able to answer something
because she had not clenched her tongue; without
another word he had deftly found the side-door lock—
as though he had done this before.

He was near her in the water; he treaded water but
she could stand squarely on the bottom of the pool. The
headlamps of a passing automobile ran footprints of
light up the tile walls. By now their eyes said everything
in the translucent darkness: their faces, their arms, their
hands were vaguely luminous on the surface of the
water. At the far side of the pool, waves from his male
splashing overflowed the troughs.

–Race you to the end, she said, for she realized suddenly he was very near. She said this to keep up the pretense they were somehow children on a lark, and this
pool was really daylight, public, and there could be no
trouble about breaking and entering.

She pushed off, her thin legs in crawl or trudgen, her
face floating sideways on the water. She did her crabbed
sidestroke, one long arm systematically breaking upward
from the water, steering her face towards the deepest
end of their pool.

He swam along beside her for a moment, a choppy
overhand motion, his legs tired, feet and knees thrash-
ing the water. His extended cheeks floated behind her
like a pair of inflated, small water wings. If they let
down now, there would be no bottom. They stopped
side by side, their fingers clinging to the gutter of the
pool, their bodies suspended in the deepest water.

–Lordy, she said. I'm not up to it. I'm not, really.

–Sure, he told her, to confirm that she was having
fun. You got to break yourself in to it.

They moved once in unison when a tide wallowed
below the night-green surface of the pool. She felt the

current grating her ankles, so she said what she had secretly feared: it's safe here?

–Sure, I got a key last year. When this building was the reserve library. The old reading room is right above us. I come here about every night. Ah, by myself.

Playfully he swelled his cheeks with air. The top of his submerging head was a boulder, or a lump of glistening quartz, disappearing below her, down into the underbrush, the waving thyme below the surface.

Left alone she gripped her tile ledge and tried to see if anyone else were in this low-vaulted room, perhaps on the entrance stairs. She could see their clothes: two dark toadstools in the shadows. Lights from the cars passing caressed the surface of the pool; the current from his submerged threshing legs sent a beast of current around her knees. She felt her legs move imperceptibly, like the tail of some indigo, tropical fish trembling in bubbles.

She saw his head, rising, a patch of light below the surface; his hands searched upward, blindly grasping the ledge. His face broke the water, and small cascades drained from the gutter of his eyes.

She thought about the half-wet condition of her hair. Then, before he blinked, she thrust herself down deep in the green water almost below him; she felt much like an animal trying to hide in a thicket of seaweed kelp.

The water pushed into her left ear. Always she had feared to swim under water. Yet now she shoved herself away from the side of the pool; for a second she was suspended, her short dark curls and her panties leaving, then clinging rhythmically to her body.

She relaxed. She arched her belly. She felt herself buoyed upward—slowly, slowly—rising as though by virtue of her own body she could float upward to the surface of his eyes.

This motion upward was so languid and so warm she did not cross her legs under the water; she allowed them to dangle apart. This upward floating, she knew absolutely from the science courses was only from air in the lungs.

When she blinked, then wiped her own eyes, he was gone. He had pulled himself, with much effort, up and over the edge of the tank. He was standing above her, reaching back down to pull her up beside him. He knew this was the moment to do what he had planned to do since he had first seen her in the graduate stalls.

He had planned, had flirted with her, had carried her books like a school boy; he had laughed too heartily and had been a stolid man in a seersucker suit all this session. Now he would pull her up over the edge of the pool. Then he would lie down. He would stretch full length on those warm tiles. She would lie back, her body shedding the clairvoyant water of the pool. Here in the dim lights when the pool was quiet from their water play, by the furtive illumination of the lights of the automobiles, he would sit upright beside her. He would pasture his eyes upon her. He would feel not the slightest compulsion to touch her. He would not take off the panties. Not really, or at least this time; he knew—really—she would not let him. But he would stare at her while she rested and while she dried. He was certain absolutely she would not mind if he only looked at her. In fact he knew she would keep her eyes closed to avoid entanglement. This one time he would see a woman, naked, thin; not like home where the wife—an obese former Sociology major—led Girl Scouts. He would stare tenderly at this unclothed woman; in this she would understand him perfectly.

He grasped her hand. He pulled her dripping up the edge of the pool. She stood dripping beside him, holding her head to one side, hammering her fist urgently against her clogged-up ear.

The beam of the flashlight shone from the entrance. The light bounded along the edge of the pool like a bloodhound. The light caught their feet, turned their shins and knees to marble. The light wavered, snuffled them, then blinded their eyes.

–All right, the watchman called in a surly, rolling voice. Come here. We'll have a good look atcha.

She would have cried. She wanted only to wake up. She was surprised at Ernest's calm. He said it in an auditorium voice that always quiets an eighth-grade assembly.

–Take that light out of my eyes—or I'll fall in again.

At the voice of command, the light wavered, lowered to their feet. She walked along beside and behind Ernest. She realized suddenly he was much shorter than she was, with his shoes off.

She was afraid: she already saw the arrival of a police car, being booked; disciplinary action from the Dean of Women; an entry on the transcript of her credits; 21 July, naked in pool.

They walked back along the edge of the tank.

The watchman on the stairs shined his light on the floor ahead of them. She began to chatter in the teeth. Then she began to watch only the hair on the calf of Ernest's leg, or his plodding foot upon the tiles.

As they walked to their towels, Ernest scooped them up. In the darkness hastily he threw a towel around her shallow waist. Fiercely he pulled it tight, a girdle. Without having to be told, she walked behind him. They were now at the foot of the steps. The night watchman again shined his flashlight directly in their faces. Everything became still.

Ernest motioned with his hands and the light obediently pointed to the wall beside them.

–Well now, the watchman said, and his timeclock swinging from its strap around his shoulder picked up reflected light on its chrome case.

–What have I caught me here?

–I been sitting up here. I been *watching* you two. My orders are to admit high-school students on Tuesday and Saturday mornings for classes in Life Saving. Otherwise, locked.

Ernest let him talk. At the foot of the steps he felt the resentment, the contempt he always felt for men older than himself who were not—as this watchman—in either a dignified or responsible position.

–We have permission, Ernest said—as though this were a fact.

–Ha! From the higher ups? He said this as a man speaks who believes he is never told of any administrative change promulgated by the Department of Buildings and Grounds. I'll best see it. In writing. No, I'd best call out our campus patrol.

–I mean, I've got a key to the building. I, ah, we been using this pool all summer. Thinking it was okay. Isn't it?

–Anyone can get a key, the old man said bitterly. Damn me, *anyone* can get a key.

–Well, we are leaving now. If you don't want us in here, Dad, we are going. You know that.

This sudden humbleness and the implication of authority swayed the old man's judgment. He had been walking his rounds for twenty-three years; he knew how much trouble it was to report anything—aside from fire. He had reported this and that, his first years, and had been made a liar out of so often he trusted only reports about fires. A fire no one could contradict—and bring witnesses; in a fire you had charred wood, and smoke damage.

–But I could get in trouble. Not reporting, hey? He shined the light up and down Ernest's flabby pink body, his square balding head.

–Yer buddy, he yaren't saying much. Step out yrear.

Ernest stepped aside, exposed her. The flashlight picked out clearly the overly long black hair on her legs, the knotted towel which concealed her panties. The glare rested squarely on her absolutely flat chest. There were no breasts. Only red welts. Her hair had been parted by the water when he pulled her from the tank. The hairs under her nose were clearly visible; all her powder was washed away. She was glad now to have her arched, ugly nose, and she was too frightened to speak.

The light snapped off. She was in darkness.

–I said we are going now. Suppose I just give you my key. To show we won't pull this stunt again.

–Hell-fire, you two boys know anybody, just *anybody* can get a key around here. Don't turn it in to me. Turn it in where you got it.

Ernest saw the old watchman's spectacles glisten in the momentary glare of passing car lights. This man was not a seeing watchman; he was a watchman primarily to smell fire.

–But mind you. The watchman stopped suddenly at the top of the stairs and gave them his light again. Then he turned with the irritability of a person who has never been able to leave gracefully, or on time, but always thinks of one more thing to say.

–For a minute I thought I'd caught me a swimming party. I found that once. Called the cops. I done that one once.

He was gone, stomping through the darkness, hurry-ing to reach his next station on time, where in some cranny a key to his timeclock hung by a chain. He would fumble for it, insert the key into the barrel of the clock around his shoulder; thus he marked the tape inside the clock for some official now asleep.

She slipped on her cotton print dress and her white shoes and picked up her own books. Without a word, they left by the side entrance, were again walking along the street between tennis courts towards the campus river and her dormitory.

Ernest fussed with the damp towels and his briefcase.

–He never came around before. I . . .

She walked, said nothing. She thought only of her dormitory, and of her room just off a third-floor hallway.

–You have to talk to those people, he said, and because she had always tried to be a good sport she replied, You sure did, you turned him off.

Even when she knew she was safe, she felt ashamed to have been inspected, to have been caught in that decrepit light. The red spots beneath her dress which were all the breasts she had been given burned as though that nascent, chilled flesh had absorbed the watchman's stare. More than anything, she wished to return to her own room, and to take a warm shower.

As she walked faster, she wanted to feel exploited, used, bereft, but she did not and could not feel what she thought was expected of her. Instead, she felt only the lucky resentment of all escape. Behind the watchman's light she sensed the surveillance of all high-school principals, of PTAs, and of her own Teachers' Union officials who always wanted more pay for everyone, but did not wish to rock any boats, as they said in committee meetings.

Worse, she felt the caricature of it. When caught, when exposed, she had been the total opposite of all those commercial models with their Jane Fonda bodies and their expensive hair and their overly long, embarrassing breasts, always stretched out on white carpets or on sheets of silk, but never on white, illicit tiles of an abandoned, locked-up university pool.

He tagged further behind, yet followed to the footbridge, shifting his briefcase from one hand to the other.

–I hope you don't. For the world I wouldn't have . . .

She stopped, knew she was walking too fast, walking away from nothing at all. Beneath an overhead light, on the center-span of the campus footbridge, she faced him.

–I don't give a good god-damn. He thought I was one of your boys.

He wanted to touch her arms, to let her know he wouldn't have had this happen for the world. He was thinking his way around some thicket of apology, and yet he wanted her to say it was all right, that he had brought it off, had saved her—and himself.

In her patient, not-quite anger, in her feeling of incapacity, she did not sense that beneath this footbridge the river was in mud flats, at the pool-stage of summer, and yet nevertheless stretched back through counties of darkness to the benumbed willow roots, to the winter drifts of her childhood.

She turned from him and walked on. By the time she saw the lighted glass of her dormitory entrance and the dutyperson at the reception desk, she was calm. The cement lions guarding the dormitory entrance seemed more inert than usual, balls of old student chewing gum for eyes.

To one side of the lions, near the irregular backwash of the hedge, he said, Good night. Wouldn't have had this thing happen for a million, you know that.

She said, Yes.

As he walked away, she knew this summer session

was finished; she would avoid him this final week of classes. Even so, she knew she would return here, or someplace like it, to earn graduate credits, a raise in pay. And then he was gone, headed back across the footbridge.

Up in her room, after her shower, she thought back upon it and laughed a little, even though in the future, when she walked past the tennis courts and that building, she would remember the watchman's roving light until that old gymnasium was condemned and at last demolished.

For one moment, in her own room, she considered again what might be wrong with her, for she had wished, for one moment while standing in the watchman's light, to rip off the towel and to betray them all.

But that moment and the now-receding echoes of her shame passed. She stood for a moment before the full-length mirror, saw only what she had always seen, and even though some shark's illicit nose might now be hammering the deadlights of some sunken hulk off Barbados, she felt something beyond the safety of graduate credit and all school boards had gone away, was now perhaps stranded downstream on the clay banks of this season.

Inside a Budding Grove

23 Suddley Avenue

Professor Gilbert Hannel Puce
Department of English
Prankins College, U of P
New Haven, Conn.

Dear Tuffy:

This time of year, as "The Bard" says, finds me with choirs aplenty but—alas—too few sweet birds. I envy you the brilliant autumn "back East" and wish I could share it with you.

But to the problem: my son, Thomas Stearns, is now entering the Senior year of what, out here, we call "High School." Essentially Tommy is a good kid, of course, but he doesn't exactly take after his Old Man in ways which Merle and myself most approve. Had any problem like that with your Suzy?

Anyway, Tommy always holed up in our basement during our regular music hours. He always showed a real flair for things mechanical. Why he has had engines and white rats in the basement since he was a child; he used to "operate" on the rats, playing Science, I guess. Now Tommy is six feet tall and weighs about two hundred. He got the motorcycle before I knew about it, but of course I was glad to find out he was rebuilding that old automobile. I admit it: the damned thing runs. As to intellect, Tommy did start out as a "slow reader" but Merle kept after him and now he has read all through Shakespeare and Chaucer and those boys, and likes 'em.

Now: in looking through your catalogue, Tuffy, I notice there are some tuition scholarships. I wonder if these are sometimes awarded on a basis of geographical distribution? Also, which men in your department serve on the Selection Committee?

Naturally Tommy is set on being an English major, though I daresay you might not find him quite up to snuff—with *your* standards—for you "Advanced Crit. Intro"—still, T. S. might make a good student, later.

If Tommy knocks off one of your tuition things, Merle and myself could very well spend next year in Italy. I'd like to get at the project that Guggenheim turned down again. In Italy I'd really dig into Castelvetro. *There* was a Critic.

My best to your "gode wif" and all of yours. Glad to hear, indirectly, that your Suzy got married. Who was it?

Oh yes, if you hear of a Department that needs a Middle-English man, let me know. I find California very d-u-l-l.

Yep, still hear from Turnball: no like him.

> Yr Obedient Ser,
> Calvin Farkesgill
> Associate Professor, English

23 Suddley Avenue

Professor Graecae Hannibal Turnball
Department of Classics
Templeton University
Huget, Georgia

Dear Hann:
   This time of year finds me with all Gaul still divided—
alas—and life continues its irregular paradigm. I envy
you the brilliant autumn which you always enjoy in the
South and I wish I could share it with you.
   Tommy [Thomas Stearns, whom you will remember
from the delightful year we spent on your campus—just
old enough then to throw croquet balls at police cars] is
now a big boy. Bigger than his old man: five-eleven and
one ninety. Isn't your Clara a year younger? Anyway,
Tommy is just finishing "High School" but I must say
he never was passed through the early discipline which
makes a classicist so very fine, like yourself—or a
Middle-English man, for that matter.
   An interesting mind, has Tommy. I mean not an outstanding mind, but an *interesting* one. He has a nice
combination of energy and a real flair for putting things
in their proper operating order. I haven't run him
through the aptitude tests—don't need to—but Merle
and I both think T. S. would make a swell linguist. God
knows we need 'em, with USSR and all; otherwise what
happens to the classics? Pretty much on his own he's
been through Shakespeare and Chaucer. And of course
he has heard a lot of music around the house.
   Now: I just happened to glance through Templeton's
catalogue. What about those Bob Jones, Jr., Out-of-State
grants? Do you sit with the committee, or anything like

that? What I really want is for Tommy to get some real discipline, and to live in a *cultured* community. Don't worry about him and segregation. He knows all about *that* . . . been through it with the wetbacks out here.

Hann, if we could finesse the tuition at Templeton for Tommy, that would see Merle and myself in "Merrie England" and once there I could clean up my Arthurian puzzle and the Roman influence for once and for all. ACLS, incidentally, didn't see eye-to-eye with us about that grant . . . going to try a Rockefeller next.

My best to your "*Summum Bonum.*" Say, wasn't that a dilly about Puce's daughter, Suzy? How long do you suppose that was going on? Merle says—ha ha—that's easy: just count on your fingers. The gent in the case, I hear, was Puce's graduate assistant! Too bad about Scrutts's kid: flunked out of Cal Tec.

Was always sorry our visit back in '66 to your campus never came to anything: I know you did your best. If you hear of an opening in Florida, let me know. Merle can't stand California weather. Also there isn't any real classical activity in these parts.

> *Vale!*
> Cal Farkesgill
> Associate Professor

23 Suddley Avenue

Professor J. D. Scrutts
Department of Anthropology
Galpar Tec., U of D
Scaddley, Wisconsin

Dear James Dudley:
This time of year finds our barrow rifled by the latter-day California Migrations but our "culture" continues apace, and there are shards of pottery, etc., in every *arroyo*.
Actually, this note is in behalf of our sibling, Tommy. He's an entering Senior at San Salibar High. Perhaps you have heard of their "Pre-Science Junior Interne" program. Well, Thomas Stearns is right in the center of *that* and I tell you our basement, for years, has been full of arrowheads, camping stuff, etc. The kid has always been a real bug on the outdoors. Not that I blame him, of course, for this is wonderful country. Every weekend T. S. heads out for the High Sierras, and he comes back with all sorts of interesting things. Lately he's been taking a girl along, and my they do have the best time.
Oh yes, reminds me: Clara Turnball (her mother is Hann's second wife) left Broadmore and is now an airline stewardess. Also too bad about Puce's Suzy. Sins of the father, hey?
Well, anyway, I just happened to see Galpar Tec's catalogue, Jamie, and wonder if you had any information on the way they give the "Grant-in-Aid" things. I note they are for students of "high personal merit" and I believe T. S. might just qualify on that score. What I really want is for Tommy to come in contact with a first-rate mind, not just a dry-as-dust collector. Wisconsin, I well know, would provide just such an

intellectual "atmosphere." Don't suppose Tommy would be up to your "Advanced Seminar: Meta-Biotics in Azulikulan," his first year, but might later. And if Tommy hit it off with Galpar, I don't doubt you could place him "out here."

Fact is, if Tommy could sign on with you-all at Galpar, then the tuition money in pocket would see the "Old Folks" to Europe. I'm ready to find out for once and for all about the relationship of Cave Ideographs to Impalic Migrations, from the Medieval point of view, of course. Thanks for the boost on that same project with the Ford Foundation; I understand we lost out in the final round. I'll try a Guggy, next year.

My best to your Squaw and your children. I guess your eldest boy is at Cal Tec? And liking it?

Just in passing, do you know anybody in the English Department at Penn State? I understand they really need a Chairman. Not that I'd exactly want to go there but that happens to be Merle's home (Scranton). She's pressuring me to return to the womb. Also, to be honest, I find all of California d-u-l-l.

Shall we open a keg—of nails—sometime?

Cal

1020 Ketchell Terrace

Dear Puce:

Note change of address. It's a long story but I'll tell you all about it over a drink sometime.

Thanks for the help on the Tuition Scholarship at U of P . . . know you did your best. Tommy's plans are still a little up in the air. He has several things lined up.

Looks like Castelvetro simply can't be made available to the Modern Mind: no Italy for Merle and myself. I've been thinking I'll just let it cool off and later get a religious angle and try it on the Catholic-Center Foundation. Have times ever been so bad for Scholarship?

Best to the "gode wif" and Suzy and her fine twins. My, I'll bet she has her arms full!

I'm reading (for review) your "Caedmon: Hunter or Harpist." I'm giving it everything I've got, of course.

Yr Obedient Ser,
Farkesgill

1020 Ketchell Terrace

Dear Turnball:

Note change of address.

Sorry Tommy lost out in the finals on the Bob Jones, Jr., deals. Tom, very wisely it seems to me, decided to get through with his Service Obligation and maybe get out before another Grass-Fire War breaks. Tommy wants the Armored Division, but Merle and myself think free training in languages or G-2 might be more fun. Tom always did have a flair for languages. I've written our Senator and tried to put the case lucidly.

No luck on my Merrie England project. "Arthur: King or Confidence Man" was turned down cold. If foundations can think so little of basic research, with the USSR and all, then perhaps I'll just have to shelve the whole thing, *sine qua non*.

Thought you might be amused to know about Puce's kid, Suzy. She brought her twins back home. The Gent in question, he gone! Where do we go from here, sez I.

Scrutts's boy got the boot at Cal Tec, but got a Fellowship in his old man's field, Anthropology, *but* in Texas. J. D. wanted Harvard, I know.

Best to your *"Summum Bonum."* California still no good.

Vale!
Farkesgill

1020 Ketchell Terrace

Dear James Dudley:

I sincerely appreciate your effort on the "Grant-in-Aid" thing; really do. Knew you could swing it, if anyone could. Also, was happy to be of service in your son's case, and conclude it does no harm to be "well connected" at a place like Texas. Fine school. He'll like it.

You may know that our Tommy has had a "change of objective" as the educationalists put it.

To make a long story short, T. S. is finessing both college and graduate school, in favor of his Service Obligation. He has already done Basic (whatever they do there). He put in for the Armored Division but got the Quartermaster. You know any Generals in the Service branches?

Why he can't use the "Grant-in-Aid" is this: he met a grand girl, though a bit older than himself. They have a great deal in common, and that High Sierra scenery did it! Merle and myself are tickled to death, of course.

Note change of address: this girl Tommy married, just before he enlisted, had several brothers. The party before the marriage—two nights before—got out of hand. We were not home, so never got the straight of it. Tommy didn't say, but I deduce something like this: the girl has four brothers, big fellows. They dropped by our house that night on some kind of business. One thing led to another; they got to celebrating. The girl in question sided with her brothers—which is understandable— but T. S. is pretty handy with the old mitts. Soooo.

The cops got there about the same time we did. The neighbors were all watching, and someone turned the hose on everybody. But it was all in good fun. The wedding came off two days later with all hands present or accounted for and all smiles. Guess that's California for you, hey?

But you know how *sensitive* Merle is. Anyway I guess we didn't need a house now that T. S. is in Service and living with his little new bride in what they call "Off Post." In short, Merle said it was a very good time to leave the neighborhood. She found this apartment. And here we are.

Actually, I like it better in just two rooms: no yard work. My books, naturally, are in storage, so "Cave Ideographs and Impalic Migrations" will have to wait. In fact I told the Dean precisely *that.*

Actually, Jim, as the Dean told me, we value teaching a great deal "out here." You, yourself, have come around to this Wisdom: to Teach is to Live . . . something like that.

Of course I don't know about your field, but in mine the real bankruptcy of scholarship—*real* Scholarship—is too apparent in such items as, "Caedmon: Hunter or Harpist" and even Tuffy's latest, "Thomas Watson: Sage or Savage." What can one say, in print, to such tiny, forced things?

No matter, though, when the bell rings for next fall

you bet I'll be right in there eating chalk dust and "doing my damnest" to influence the Minds of This Generation. If not us, J. D., then who can do the job?
See you Christmas, at the convention!

Skoal!
Calvin Farkesgill

But Who Gets the Children?

Finally I got back to my office from Binghamton via Newark and the airport limo. I don't like airplanes any more, and that flight held at ten-grand over Matawan forty-eight minutes while a lost jet trainer tried to find Long Island somewhere beneath the cloud cover.

At our home office I got the bad news.

Also a telegram—not a telex or anything so conventional as a telephone message in our Age of Communication—a delivered telegram from Sade, my Ever Loving.

BRING MOLLE SS RING GASKET FITTINGS SS
SINK TWENTY ONE BY THIRTY . . . LOVE

I love my wife a lot, I really do. Sade was once at Wright Field, Dayton, Ohio. Sade's government thing about telegrams still hangs on. Or perhaps Sade knew I might "forget," then lie to her. That's happened.

At the plumbing-supply house a man said SS meant

stainless steel, a rim for a sink, and also it meant $22.32 out the door.

To me it also meant Sade was working again on our kitchen.

Oh I love my wife, so after three weeks on the road I put this square, stainless-steel hoop around my neck, the hold-down clamps in my pocket and used both hands to fight my way to a commuter train headed home.

We live in Oyster Village, a place not even the builder thought of four years ago. We didn't want to leave the city but we have two kids. Bad kids, too; they bite.

Here is the way we got into Oyster Village in the first place.

We had to move somewhere and I thought we both liked this split level, on a corner lot. When Sade was in the hospital with Lew, Jr., I borrowed four bills to meet closing costs and signed a mortgage to surprise her. On my first visit to the hospital I said, "Ever loving baby's got that new home."

Naturally I thought it would be good news, but I can see how she might be surprised. Anyway, Sade just looked at Lew, Jr., wrapped in a blanket beside her and said, "Oh?"

Then I got it out of her. While I had been raising three bills to close, she had been planning a place that was "different." That little place was seventy miles from Goose Hawk, Connecticut. We had driven up there once and found it: mostly pasture, in one corner an old white horse; for improvements there was a barn, also this shed, and also an abandoned signboard on stilts that once advertised either snuff or a local Savings and Loan.

"What we could do," I said at the time, "is pick up a surplus missile silo and go Classic."

"Use some imagination," Sade said. "Can't we ever do something different?"

I felt sorry for her. I always do.

Sade reads a lot and with no additional training she could be one of those personal color consultants. Always, she wants us to be "different."

So do I. I want to be so different it hurts me; it really does. But to be "different" in her sense takes simply more money. Someone like me doesn't bring it home. I just don't bring home that old flight pay as I did when we met at Wright, in Dayton, Ohio. That's when I was the hottest multi-engine pilot that ever worked a tower and then landed on the wrong airfield. Not far from New Orleans, and it was easy. All of that was some years ago, and I do not like airplanes anymore. Not even on the ground.

Don't get me wrong about Sade. She can squeeze a dollar some. She sews some and exchanges baby clothes with two neighbors in Oyster Village. It's on the big things Sade still cannot believe we are only ordinary people; mostly we run in the break-down lane. That's why we are in a tract-type split-level so called. Deep down I thought it was a pretty good place, with no possibilities; Sade thought it was a bad, bad place, with no possibilities at all. But she can't keep herself from trying.

For example, furniture.

While I was on the road, I wanted Sade to have everything convenient for our new baby. I borrowed two thou to buy what we needed: used dryer, a washer, a refrig, a TV complete with antennae, and five or six floor lamps. Also a nice portable bar, with real leather. I bought the stuff from people who were stepping up to bigger houses farther out on the Island. So maybe the washer flooded if you put in detergent—mostly it was good stuff. Personally, I used the bar quite a lot when home.

When I brought Sade and Lew, Jr., back from the hospital to our new split-level in Oyster Village and all our new stuff, I thought she would like it. Sade went from the front room to the kitchen and said, "Why, yes. My, this is nice."

The old stiff upper lip. You know, American Lips, modified, can take it.

Finally I got it out of her. While I was acquiring all this stuff on the side, to surprise her, she was planning something different: we should buy one thing at a time and get matched appliances and Hi-Fi-and-Video; go "quality" to make up for our conventional split-level house. Meanwhile we live on orange crates and sweat our payment. Was Sade right? You tell me.

I did what anyone would do: tried to make it up to her.

I led her over to the window and pointed along the street. The roofs of the other houses were just like ours; viewed together the roofs were asbestos shingle stair steps, rising up the grade on both sides of the street. We were no different from the others. Everyone on Long Island is trying to make it from day to day; against this we have to understand each other, and work out the problems. Besides, I had only wanted to surprise her. She said, "Yes, Lew," and seemed to mean it.

I tried to kid her a little: "The natives are restless tonight," I said, and pointed to the ascending stairway of the roofs. "Soon our work here will be done. Then, back to civilization!"

I don't know what Sade said because Lew, Jr., began to cry.

I made a pitcher of Martinis, but there was no vermouth in the house. That suited me fine, so I celebrated two pitchers worth of our happy homecoming.

Okay, so I'm a bum, married to a nice girl and have a secret vice or something. Right? Well, let me give you my side of it. I'm thirty-six, five feet eleven, etc. Three weeks out of every month I cover Vermont, New Hampshire, New York State, except for the big accounts, and Maine. I "call on" people, as we say; I fly United and Republic Air, and I know some of the captains. I use rent-a-car services. I'm in motels all week, and some of them are real hot-pillow joints. Sometime try Watertown, New York, on a Thursday. It's expensive, but Simmons H & G has only six cars on lease and I don't rate one.

Yes, I said Vermont. I sell hose and tubing, extruded stuff, and it is a very fine product because J. Q. Simmons makes every foot of it "hisself." That's what he tells us.

Oh, it's very good hose. But his product can't really stand modern, high-pressure systems. So I hit canning factories that operate only three months in season, rickety sewing lofts, and a few pulp plants. All those managers tell me the same thing: 1) closing down for the season; 2) closing down because of "taxes"; 3) closing down. New England is a bad territory. It's getting worse.

Three weeks of that, and I get a week "at home." On those days, naturally, I go into the city to our main office. When I am really at home, at night, there is always something to repair, like the washing machine. Fun with the wife and kids, they tell me.

Here is the thing: while I am on the road, Sade remodels. She does-it-herself. First she reupholstered everything in the front room and painted the walls in coral and lime green and hung lamps from the walls. ". . . Like it, dear?"

Then our dining room: she put iron legs under the tables; everything that was dark became blond oak; she made drapes with tropical fish the size of your head. ". . . Like it, dear?"

Now the kitchen: this one could be bad.

Don't get me wrong. Sade really has improved our house and I give her credit. Also, I understand exactly why. Sade is lonely and a little frightened every night for three long weeks before Her Hero gets home. She paints and sews and refinishes to keep from thinking, to arm herself against being lonely. Isn't that awful?

That's why I played along and picked up the SS rim for $22.32 and hipped it through the crowds to make my train.

At O.V. no one met me at the station—of course. I knew Sade couldn't get away at that hour because of the kids. She always makes it if she can. I walked two miles to save cab fare.

Well, our kitchen looked like a mad bomber slept here. The wall next to the garage was demolished; you looked out into the bare garage walls where the garden hose was coiled. This was no do-it-yourself project. Where the stove had been there was now a half-finished dining booth of white leatherette. Our new appliances eventually would fit into an "appliance wall."

"Where's the bar?" I said. "Should have a bar?"

Sade pointed to the hole in the kitchen wall.

"Playroom *and* bar in the garage," she said, but all I could see was a fender with a dent the size of a collie dog. I'd already spent the insurance company's check, but the fender was rusting.

"Where do we keep the car? This winter?"

"New carport," she said. Sometimes when she pulls stuff like that I take out my wallet and pull out all my credit cards to show her how it is. When I did the old wallet routine, Sade began to cry. She just folded up and bawled and bawled.

I put my arms around her, and finally she stopped crying. She wished she had not started such a big job but it was supposed to be finished when I got home . . . Surprise.

I tried to be understanding; I really did. But tonight seemed too much until I realized it was mostly my fault. For example, if I'm in New Hampshire, or Watertown, I call long distance about every night. I ask for Mr. Fugit or Mr. Simplex and Sade says, "He's expected here tomorrow."

That's how we kept in touch.

Some nights, depending on the operator, Sade hears my voice. We know everything is all right. I always feel sorry for her when I hang up without speaking to her. If I were home more, things would be different.

"The carport is on the same loan from the builder who sold us the place," she said. "But do you *like* it, honey?"

"Like it fine," I said, and I kissed her again and said I'd keep an eye out for a job that paid more and that we could make it just fine. . . .

Sade stopped calling herself a fool; she began to feel better.

Then I said in a real cheerful voice, "This calls for a drink."

Nearly everything did when I was home.

We did not have anything in the house to drink, so I got in the car and found a package store. When I got home there were candles lighted on a cake. It was my birthday. I had forgotten all about that.

Naturally, just then I could not tell Sade the bad news: fired.

Not exactly dismissed: the "territory" simply folded up under me, like an old horse that has carried its last load. When I got in from Binghamton I was surprised to find that not only was I out of a job but that Simmons Hose & Gasket was on the block. The company would make a nice tax loss for some other outfit.

I did not tell Sade the bad news right then. After the children were in bed, we sat around and had a few. After that things looked better, as though we were both very young and on flight pay. See how happy we can be, sometimes?

Next day I went into the city to look for a job. Did you ever walk into a huge building, a strange building, where no one could possibly want to see you? It's a creepy feeling, even at noon in midtown New York City.

I'd never really looked for a job before. When I got home from the hospitals, I got this position with Simmons H & G without a struggle. Now I know a lot of people in the business, but everyone I knew was also waiting in those same outer offices. I saw this one was going to be tough.

Finally I headed back to Oyster Village. I intended to break the news to Sade at 6:55 upon arrival. I never made it to the station. On the way I ran into Wendy Robartes.

I had not seen Wendy for three months. We used to fly out of Travis. Sometimes we met at Wake. In New York we keep in touch because Wendy is also a Midwesterner. He's chubby now, and still blond: he never married, and is a four-color pressman and spills half of it.

Naturally we stopped to talk only a minute; naturally we stepped into this bar naturally.

When I told Wendy I could not have another, he looked surprised.

So I told him: "I'm headed for O.V., to tell Sade the bad news."

"What we *need*," he said, and winked and slapped me on the back, "is a . . ."

I said, "Our natives, Sir Hardwick, seem restless tonight."

So we went up to Wendy Robartes' apartment. Wendy called in a buddy but I never did catch the name. The three of us sat around and shot the breeze about the old days. You know how it goes: whatever happened to Teddy and Camel and Saddle-Sore Kelly. . . .

Then I told them how I lost the best damn air crew in the USAF.

"So *after* they bailed out," and Wendy had heard this one, "you never did see any of them again. Right?"

"Two engines," Wendy's buddy said, who had not heard this one before. "On fire. Inland. From the Coast?"

"I couldn't count the chutes. I was in the cockpit."

"But someone later reported ten chutes?"

"Was ten everybody?" Wendy's buddy said, "I mean . . ."

"That's-question," I said. "Which two didn't get out?"

"So never saw any of them? Ever?"

"No, but five years ago I got a Christmas card from a vet's hospital from the Tech Sergeant. He didn't know anything either, but he heard only eight chutes got reported."

So we had a drink on that.

Okay, okay, okay.

Well, we scoped it out: go out to our place, to Oyster Village. Open one and see if there's a pearl, Wendy's buddy said, and I said, I want you to see Sade's remodeling deal.

Okay, okay, okay.

So tomorrow we get up early at O.V. Have some eggs. Pitch in. Do the damned job . . . finish the old house . . .

Then I *sell* the house. Profit *before* first payment's due.
Okay, okay, okay.
Ra-jah!
Anyway, I wanted Wendy to meet Sade. Really did.
"Should I take our little friend?" says Wendy.
Our little friend was a bottle of whiskey. We took it along to the car.
Okay, okay, okay, okay.
We lost Wendy's buddy on the way to Oyster Village. Maybe he decided to fly this mission in the Gent's Room. Anyway, we couldn't find him when we left the last tavern, so Wendy drove his car out on the parkway. By then we were singing, *"Oh happy is the day when the airman gets his pay and we go rolling, rolling home . . ."*
We made it on to O.V., and Wendy got the gear down and locked and full-flaps on our lawn and we walked away from it.
Sade was gone. So were the kids. There was a note that read like a telegram:

CALLED OFFICE. YOU FIRED. AT STATION
MEET YOU. LOVE.

Now I would not have to tell her, but I would have to tell her why I didn't tell her before.
I knew why Sade had the kids in the automobile at the station at midnight. She thought I'd need help getting off the last train. But I didn't. I was home, but she wasn't. We had missed connections again.
I explained that to Wendy. He laughed and laughed and you can see how funny it was.
"Moderne," I said, and showed Wendy the front room and the dining room and the kitchen.
"A mad bombardier slept here," I said and Wendy laughed and sat down on the kitchen floor.

Then I saw through the hole in the wall and into the empty garage beyond.

I jumped through the hole in the kitchen wall and got the ax.

"You like moderne?"

Wendy did not answer. He was asleep.

"I'll remodel good," I said, "because the Na-tives are restless . . ."

I started in on the kitchen cabinets. Ever tear anything down? Something painted and full of dishes and glasses and cups and trays? I was swinging the big double-bitted ax like a prop blade. Everything in the kitchen began to fall.

I went into the dining room. I chopped the corners off of everything that was square. I got the bathroom door. I got the living room and got the pictures and all hanging lamps.

Then I saw Sade standing in the door her mouth like this.

I was glad she was home. For a minute I had thought she was leaving on the train. Now she was back. I really was glad to see her because I could not make that laughing ax blade stop. I watched the ax laugh upward, high above my head, and then the baby's high chair down the middle.

Cop.

He was standing in the other door. He had a notebook in his hand. He could not believe what he was seeing: the laughing ax blade. Split everything in the house.

By that time Wendy was up. He was laughing. Then he stopped.

Then I stopped when the cop said, "Out in front. Would that be a stolen car?"

Wendy's buddy reported we stole his car. That's why the cop walked in.

"Maybe you both better come with me," the cop said.

He took the ax out of my hand and stepped through the wall into the garage and hung it up again.

Sade didn't say anything. She was looking at her former house. She tried to cry. Then she ran over and threw her arms around me.

"Don't take him," she said. "He's not himself."

Actually I tried to talk the cop into taking me. I wanted to go. "I am myself," I yelled. "It's me. I'm always this way."

I pointed to the wrecked kitchen and the wreckage of her plans and my plans and our plans and of all my weeks away in Vermont and all the bad hose and bad gaskets and bad management and too many bills and too many drinks.

Okay, okay, okay. . . .

"No, you are not," Sade told me. She grabbed and held me. "He's sick. He's tired."

"Yes," said the cop and began to write in the notebook. "That's what a lot of them tell me."

"My fault," Sade said. "I ran up all those terrible bills. He was alone every night up in Maine, and . . ."

"That's what a lot of them tell me, all right."

"Oh, it's not his fault, officer. Lew was hit. He couldn't bail out. Everybody else did, but he went down with the airplane. They found him floating."

Just then our baby began to cry. Lew, Jr., was in the back seat of the car. You could hear him through the open hole in the kitchen wall.

The cop stepped over all that debris and walked back through the hole in the kitchen wall. He looked into the car. The baby was crying louder, but our little girl was asleep through it all.

"If you won't," the cop said, meaning about charges, "then I won't. Tonight."

Sade put her arms around me, as though I had never been away.

That was enough for the cop. He took Wendy out to the patrol car; I said tomorrow, some way, I'd post the bail.

I was tired. I sat down at the table—what was left of the table—as though I were going to eat a meal. I thought, then, I would sleep. But I only cried.

There never are any tears when a man cries, but your shoulders rise up and down and up and down as though they will never stop.

"Home," I heard her say. "Home . . ."

I didn't know whether Sade meant home, here in Oyster Village, or if she meant home, in Toledo, Ohio, where we both came from. Her parents still live there.

But she said it again and again with one arm around my neck because now she also was crying.

"Home," she said. "Let's go home . . ."

The Snow Hunter

Before dawn, face wrapped in cloth against this third snow of November, the hunter went past the town's outermost, now unguarded, barricade. The hunter held to the creek bank past an abutment of poured concrete, encased in snow, the top not visible in the dark, a thing which once held up either railroad tracks or the highway going West.

Among the first scrub oaks the track became only a boot-sole wide. The sky lightened, confirmed the territory ahead: sea heaves of purple snow where the hills rose.

His back to fresh wind, the hunter took the rifle from his shoulder. He inspected the stock. The clip had but two shells remaining. He allowed something for windage with his rear sight. In the valley behind him, their town was now a square irregular shadow. The hunter made out almost certainly the chimney smoke from the fire he, himself, built in their fireplace to benefit his sleeping wife and the girl—not their own daughter.

That fire-builder moment stayed in the hunter's mind:

a flame taking firelogs. Very much he wished for his wife and the girl to sleep past daylight until his return and thereby to be neither hungry nor alone in their log-reinforced house.

The memory of a flame between crossed firelogs caused the hunter to turn at once into the wind, to walk through the silent brush. His wrapped head and face and his old overcoat became a more deliberate shadow; he moved without sound except that of boot rags catching the stalks of dead weeds.

In the half-light, where the track became a promontory of stone, the hunter stopped, felt this day's arrival was timed well, sensed the snow and the wind fall into the scrub oaks at his back.

Above the far rim of this larger valley the sun rose; the bend of the creek was a fracture of willows among drifts. As the hunter stared, the drifts on the valley floor for one instant seemed to become a leaping deer of fire—was gone.

The illusion of a fire-deer leaping passed. The hunter began to watch more intently the bend of the creek where water rippled in the light.

From near the creek, from beneath snow-laden branches, the hunter saw a man emerge. The man walked out into the sun.

This man wore a scrub-colored overcoat, head and face wrapped against the cold. The gait was steady, a shuffling motion: walked on some kind of bark and bent-branch snowshoes. His traps of wire and rope swung across his back, a trapper.

Beside the riffles, the trapper stopped. The trapper turned his back to the wind. He hesitated, looked for something. Looked again for something, then found it. The trapper pulled a trap from the creek bank. He had taken something grey, something frozen, a small block of fur-covered ice.

The trapper shook ice from the grey pelt. Suddenly, startled, the trapper looked up, stood taller, seemed to push himself back, as though getting up from a table.

Only then, from above, did the hunter hear the reverberating, sharp, winter sound. One shot.

The trapper fell.

In one moment, as though having waited a brief interval to see if there were to be further movements, two men—one tall, one short—came like shadows from beneath nearby, snow-covered willows.

From his escarpment, the hunter recognized the small man, for the hunter previously had agreed to meet the small man on this day and at this place.

By the time the hunter walked down into the valley, to the riffles of the creek, the two men had taken most things of value from the trapper, had arranged these things in three equal piles.

–We saw you up there, the small man said. Only his intelligent, brown eyes were visible above the wraps across his face; his voice was conversational, informative; the breath of his speech came through the face cloth and hung for a moment in the cold, a white cloud of words.

As always, the hunter noted the small man was in good flesh, was eating very well—someway.

"I thought you might still be in bed . . ."

–We came out here last night, the tall man said, and his gun was cooling rapidly, smelled of blue cordite. We snow-camped.

"So that's why I saw no tracks at all?"

–He didn't see no tracks neither, the small man said, and gestured with his face wraps towards the dead trapper in the snow.

"Had he come on across," the hunter said, as though to confirm his rights in this one, "I would have took him. From my side."

–Yes sir, the tall man said, and he kept moving in the way of a new associate who is trying to be all right.

–Sure, sure, the small man said easily through his face wraps. This one *about* on time. This morning.

Without lost motion, the tall man whose gun was now totally cooled, rolled the body of the trapper face up to get at the knife—maybe two—from the inside overcoat pockets. When the head rolled over in the snow, the face wraps came loose.

The wound was very good, almost precisely through the left eye: a head shot. The head shot had caused the trapper to stand a little more upright in the sun for one moment.

–Why he's black, the tall man said, who was a new associate. With the upper jacket cut away, to be used later for boot rags, it was evident: this was a black man, someone strong enough to go a long way on his very efficient snowshoes. A Negro for sure, possibly once from a city, who had for some reason come West.

–From—I'd say—considerable . . . and the small man seemed not at all surprised that the trapper was black. From considerable distance. Up-river. From here.

While the tall man was throwing everything of no value into the underbrush by the creek, and also while he was binding the arms and legs with the trap wires so the trapper would freeze solid and in that way, at spring thaw, become useful again for flesh bait, the short man motioned the hunter to step aside, to speak in confidence behind a snow-covered cluster of willows.

–I am giving you a draw, the small man said. Six more shells for your clip.

The hunter hesitated, then remembered the flame

rising suddenly from two firelogs on the hearth; he held out his hand and then put the six shells furtively into a side pocket of his overcoat.

"You don't have to give me a draw. A deal is a deal."

–Oh, I had some luck, and the smaller man winked. Among a wide circle of acquaintances. In the city. Up-river.

"I know that," the hunter said, and heard his own voice become respectful.

The small, intelligent man loosened his face wraps, the easier to speak.

–That girl, and the small man was more confidential. Would I still be able to take her off your hands? Come summer?

For one moment the hunter looked beyond the valley rim, as though he detected some movement among the scrub. As he had done before and as he would do while he worked with this man whom he had known for a long time for they were both born and both grew up in the village, as he did because the smaller man had moved out, had left, had traveled very carefully for long distances to the cities, and to the East, the hunter nodded, "Yes, a deal is a deal."

–That's why I had Walter throw something extra in your pile. For the girl.

Whereupon they made arrangements for another meet, at another time and another place—weather permitting.

On the way home beneath a new, wet snowfall, the hunter held to the cutbank path, his new snowshoes taking him easily past the tilted abutment, now bonewhite, encased totally in new snow.

"Rabbit," was what the hunter said to his wife and to the girl—not their daughter. Not their own daughter, who once had gone out with other small girls for a little walk and who would now never return to this log-reinforced house.

"Rabbit," he said, the fire in the fireplace brightly aflame.

"I got up," his wife said, and she understood the hunter had done it again, had returned with a great deal of meat, enough for three weeks.

"I got up as you left—but let her sleep."

The girl had the largest knife and was already taking the skin from the rabbit which had been hanging from the trapper's waist beneath his overcoat.

In the Valley of
the Kilns

In these mountains, our flight together now past, I understand more clearly a return to the valley of my youth and to its factories might signify reconciliation and might be even wise; yet, against that compromise, I face again the ultimate fact of my wife now dead, and also two children. A sentimental gesture of return to the quarries can only dishonor love's memory.

In this cave, therefore, I shall remain and here I shall die.

Before the death by falling (boy), by deadfall (girl), or her death (broken heart), I understood only a little the price of our rebellion. What I had not fully understood until now is how little our crime changed even slightly the established quotas of work, or the products of clay which at this moment are being fired, tallied, and cooled each week and each quarter of every year.

In the Valley of the Kilns our names are not recorded.

To the thousands of workers who remain, our flight so long ago signifies nothing. Were I to return to the

Valley for trial, would public confession of error perpetuate her memory? I doubt it.

Nevertheless, I make this chronicle of two lives accurate with neither apology nor self-delusion intended. And as I set down these words which never shall be read, farther back in this cave I hear the great clay heart of the world beating darkly among stalactites.

At dawn, when the snowfields above wink in the first light, I foresee clearly my own fate: extinction by wolves when I can no longer walk for fuel. Until then I accept austerely the seasons remaining. Toward evening, I watch deer walk from the forest near my deadfalls to drink; at times, when the rains of winter come, my certain end may seem almost just. If by chance, in the future, someone reads these mere words on paper, no doubt they will make other judgments: each reader for himself alone.

Although in the Valley the routine of each morning is the same, I recollect vividly my first day of duty on the high escarpments.

Before the first rays of the sun illuminated the peaks, I was awake. In the farthest reaches of our barracks-caves, I heard hundreds of workers stirring, coming towards the light to work. Outside, the first "music" from the loudspeakers flooded our flat, wide, white assembly area.

Across the Plaza, on the front porches of their individual dwellings, precisely at the same moment, our Foremen appeared. In a stately way, all in a line, they walked across the Plaza.

As the sun rose, our crews stood at attention.

Fascinated, we listened to the roll call of production units; then yesterday's work done, and this new day's communal goals. With great excitement each morning I heard the tonnage for Escarpment-Six. With one voice we pledged Fidelity to the Kilns: our work to be pure, to uphold the customs of our craft, to sacrifice, etc., etc. My voice with a thousand other voices re-echoed our pledges upward into the sun's first rays. And I was young.

Therefore I accepted the high escarpment where the clay was talcum white. From those heights our kilns seemed only brown-smoke hives no larger than a wineskin. We blasted great avalanches of rock which fell like a long white feather of rolling thunder towards the conveyor gangs three thousand feet below.

Our work was elite work. The entire enterprise of the Valley rested upon us: without clay all kilns must cease production. The risk was great and only those with a nimble, extraordinary sense of possible catastrophe survived. On the high escarpments my character was formed, and I became a man.

Towards noon our Foreman signaled his drill crews strung out along the sheer, rising walls. We came down to his assembly area to eat and to rest for one hour.

"So: my eagles come for food?" our Foreman always said, and each day smiled at his own joke. Yet it was true; we called one another "Eagle." Because of rains or wind erosion, if an apparently solid path gave way suddenly with a hollow rush of air beneath a man's feet, we believed that man flew through space for a long time before the rolling, white-feather avalanche took him.

I saw two hundred men "fly" briefly, then disappear into tons of rock and white clay at our escarpment's base, yet not one man cried out. Instead, backs arched, arms extended and in that classic position they fell—down, down, became smaller, smaller—and at last tumbled end-over-end when the avalanche of rock took them.

Our bread, our white cheese, our customary wineskins passed from the eldest to the youngest man in our crew; vividly I remember the shapes of our brown, hairy legs as we rested beneath the shade of an overhang.

Against the talcum dust our feet were sturdily splayed; our ancestors had also worked these quarries, had climbed these escarpments of clay where dust and sky became one.

At rest time our intricately woven, encoded loin cloths breathed in the light; our loin cloths showed our future assignments, our destiny in the enterprise of the kilns. Only Foremen and upper-level Management could read those secrets; all others obsessively stared without comprehension. Besides our identical matching headbands, each man had a device implanted in the upper arm. At certain hours these devices made "music"; at others, especially at night, they merely hummed. Happily, something was listening.

When the sun setting touched the rim of the mountains, we re-formed on a lower terrace; by now our bodies had become liquid-ivory statues, breathing easily. Sometimes singing, incredibly white from the blow dust, we went at a half-trot to the Valley floor.

At the Assembly Plaza, later, especially in the windless nights of spring, the kilns seemed to become upright, mighty organ pipes, glowing in their own heat, turning orange, then red, and just before dawn, pale blue. At those moments our singing became one voice rising from the dark, open throat of the Valley.

A feeling of right order came upon us. We were at one with an enterprise which signified purpose, something essential to our larger world.

One summer night exactly like that I lay half-asleep at the entrance of our barrack-cave. Above the escarpments I watched our constellation take more perfect shape: the Great Jug with three handles; to the West, The Brick, also mighty in orbit against the vast, ultimate furnace of our universe.

"Awake?" and it was my Foreman from the escarpment, his profile a blade of cast bronze against the light of our kilns.

"My Eaglet much awake?" his tone was ironical, the customary speech of all Foremen. In the mysterious way of Management, he knew where to find me, and that I was awake.

Casually the Foreman picked up the end of my loin cloth. By holding it parallel, he shifted those patterns alongside the beads of my headband. When aligned, the two narrow sashes caught the light from the kilns, blinked, and for a moment, joined to become a larger pattern.

"What I see here . . . Eaglet—" My Foreman then held the bead patterns unnaturally close to his hooked nose. He said, "Yes, . . . "

"*Is* . . .

For the first time, I realized the man who had first led me to the escarpments was near-sighted; worse, his hesitation conveyed absolutely that he did not clearly read— could only guess—what my loin cloth and headband patterns foretold. With shock I realized, I understood the knowledge of all Foremen—and by extension all Management—was approximation, myth. Furthermore, in his moments of hesitation, my Foreman seemed incredibly old.

"Cert-ain-ly!" and I heard false enthusiasm. "She reads, 'new assignment.' Hah?"

Because I had grown to full manhood on the escarpments and had survived, I expected change; yes, and also reward and recognition. Yet because I had been taught so, at that moment I *felt* nothing at all. Thus my deeply protective reply was very much the tone of my Foreman.

"So: tomorrow is my time?"

Abruptly, he turned from me.

First he seemed an abnormally tall figure, his shadow

massive, blue; then he was only a man growing smaller as he walked almost furtively back across the Plaza.

I called out.

He did not turn back.

I trotted across the Plaza, towards the first row of little houses where the Foremen lived with their "wives." I touched his shoulder.

Fear was what I saw in his face: I had crossed their Plaza, had touched him. Because of my audacity, he drew back.

"Am I a Foreman?" I asked, "with house?"

Because all windows in all this small house were dark, I thought, *Why no one at all lives here. These are house fronts. These doors lead only to other quarters, perhaps into barracks-caves.*

Far down the production lines an extraordinary flash of blue light illuminated his face, the house fronts, and his door.

"You . . . you have done well."

"Then a wife assigned?"

In the way of all Management, he both spoke, and turned from me.

With one futile disengaging motion of arm and shoulder, he disappeared through the door.

I never saw him again.

Bent low, I trotted back across the Plaza to the place where I belonged. I felt bereaved, desolate, as though suddenly on some high, rotting escarpment I had become afraid. As I reached the safety of our barrack-cave, the device in my arm began to play softly: music for marching, and also music for sleeping.

I awoke beside Kiln 82-B.

That is to say, I came to understanding through work on our production lines. My loin-cloth patterns took me not to a small, white Foreman's house but to three years and forty days as lead-off man beside the fire doors.

Past daybreak one day in spring our crew of men entered the firing shed; at the same moment, the crew-women also arrived through their portal.

Our procedure was exact.

Each man of our crew placed carefully one molded, white-square of clay on the firing rack. The women opposite scribed the day's pattern and "fed" the clay with a brush and red-vitreous glaze. Whereupon Caliper-men measured each brick and each row of bricks, trying without rancor to find their own quota of "Second-Forms." Nimbly, within the permitted time-frame, tier-upon-tier the pallets rose as high as our tallest man could reach. For the firing run all pallets required perfect alignment.

The Talley-men, those roving jackals with clipboard and abacus, came and went; our Foreman with his symbolic, lashless whip of porcelain stood high above on his platform, never smiled.

Beyond my lead-off station, always, I was aware of the curved door of our furnace and of the fires within.

At a signal from the platform above, I rolled back our furnace doors. One crew on either side, we pushed forward the wheeled truck of perfectly aligned, unfired bricks. When the heat caused the others to fall back, I, alone, pushed the load deeper into the furnace. Then I, too, was outside. The door of the kiln slammed shut, locked.

At once we walked to the rear of that roaring kiln. We pulled forth an incandescent, square honeycomb of new bricks which glowed like the sun.

To see an aligned, glowing dolly of bricks emerge triumphant from its week-long fire made us cry out in an almost indescribable joy.

Another crew pushed that truck—glowing steadily, turning red—towards cooling yards. Always we watched the square of light grow smaller until it was only a firefly disappearing.

At such a moment we met.

I had seen her each day for three years, but because each worker inexorably was at one with our production, with the ideology of our Valley, the distinctions between men and women, while on the production lines, long ago ceased to exist.

With that distinction vanished, we spoke to one another only in quota-words, or communal song. To see another person or to touch accidentally across a pallet of clay was not at all to "meet."

As had happened before, when the last pallet of the day emerged from our kiln, I had a terrible moment of vision. Three times before when I looked into the flames, unmistakably I saw my own face. That day, however, writhing, as though sculptured in flame, I saw the outline of my whole body, complete with loin-cloth patterns.

Blind, stricken, I fell down in the blue shadow of our Whip's platform. For one moment he too was blinded by the fiery sun of new bricks emerging.

"You do . . ." was what she said very softly, her face partly averted, "More . . ."

What she said was illicit, and also not possible—that *anyone* could do "more"; yet secretly, I knew in my own heart what she dared say was true.

"More than anyone . . ."

The movements of my body had told her so: at the furnace door, then deeper into the flames than anyone else, I dared push our pallets; on the production line, at times, I was an Eagle still, high on the escarpment's most daring walls. And this, secretly, she understood.

We did not touch.

Instead, impulsively, she picked up the end of my loin cloth. Intently, she held the pattern of her loin cloth in parallel to mine. Never before had I seen a woman's hand do something so intensely female.

In the shadow of the platform above, at a moment when even the Talley-men were blinded, on shards of old brick, illicitly and contrary to Law and in the face of death by burning, she kissed me.

Terror was what I felt. The Valley suddenly seemed to tremble because of our unplanned disobedience. Then as though we had passed only in those shadows, we stood apart, stepped back into our respective lines.

In the next weeks, two things happened.

At Kiln 82-B my personal effort—a concept not before known to me—redoubled.

I pushed our piled-high carts of unfired bricks almost into the very heart of the awful flames. Secondly, in ways I had not thought possible, she managed to put glaze on almost every brick which I placed on any pallet. No word was spoken, yet our work was for ourselves alone.

And it was true: she managed to let others place her just beyond my touch, and yet I did observe her closely.

We had no names. Outwardly she was precisely as all other women I had ever seen except in the center of her black, long hair was an enigmatic skein of ash-white. When the heat of the kiln blew her hair back across her shoulders, that line of color glowed and floated as I watched.

Clearly that mark was her disqualification to bear children. Furthermore, I saw now a destructive, impulsive aspect of her work. She was wasteful of glaze, and at day's end impulsively threw down the honored tools of her craft. But would she, ever, see her own face in the consuming flame?

After six weeks we met again in the darkness beneath a Talley-man's decorated platform.

With absolute disdain for the symbolic porcelain whip above us, she said, "Tomorrow, I go down. To the cedar forests."

Even with the Talley-man directly overhead I might have cried out but she touched me, placed her blunt, short fingers across my lips.

Far down the tracks towards the cooling sheds, we saw our last dolly of bricks glowing, becoming smaller in the exceptional, somehow comforting, darkness.

Without saying anything, she turned towards the receding light, and because of love for her I took the second step. We were two shadows running, following the narrow rails onward.

Then we were going underneath vast, half-submerged sheds, their roofs held up by massive columns of brick.

Suddenly, ahead, the glowing, honeycomb of fired bricks flared, went out; the tracks had abruptly turned.

Because it was totally dark, we walked more slowly. Underfoot were shards of pottery, of brick; overhead we saw massive savagely decorated platforms where once Foremen and Talley-men austerely watched. These platforms from another age were deserted, falling down.

We emerged beneath the sky and climbed rough-hewn, primal steps to an upper platform. Stretched out ahead in the moonlight, humped like the back of some sleeping, vicious animal, I saw the roofs of cooling sheds stretching away.

In full flight, with no guide save the escarpment to the East, gradually we went towards the docks, the shipping yards.

On either side we passed between pallets of stacked-up bricks with three holes, then past canted stacks of jugs in a hundred sizes, all with three handles. Gradually these piles became smaller, the sheds more haphazard.

After four miles, the shed roofs were rotted, or blown away, the abandoned roof posts no taller than my waist. At last even the posts were only rubble, covered by silt or by clay blown here by the winds.

Beyond the last vestige of mounds, at two o'clock in the morning, we stopped. For a moment we turned, looked back.

Beneath the sky we saw blue and orange organ pipes of flame, a mosaic of streets and plazas, the row-upon-row of mighty kilns, the entire Valley a hearth glowing—the place where we were born.

Ahead was a canyon of stone, prelude to the chaos of mountains.

Listening intently, we heard the far-off, sweet, industrial hum rising from the Valley of the Kilns. We felt bereft, but we did not turn back.

What I saw next made all of the difference.

When we fled the kilns, I feared the areas of the yards, and the river docks. Here the Talley-men roved with their giant, three-eyed dogs.

These areas were central to our enterprise: our crews in the forest, on the escarpment, beside the kilns, or in the vast network of cooling sheds; yes, and our myriad of quotas, our athletic games when we ran long distances carrying heavy weights, and most especially the patterns programmed into our loin cloths.

Thus we believed: from our yards and docks—made Holy by Shardsmen—our tile and our brick moved onward to construct walls and fantastic cities high on mountain tops we had never seen. These things known were the end, the justification of all our sacrifice.

Yet here, beyond the most savage, burnt-out cooling

sheds, there were no railway yards. No docks. Where rail yards might have been, I saw only ancient, low ridges coming together. These ridges intersecting might once have been a primitive system of dikes, or canals, or possibly roadbeds—now abandoned, now overgrown.

What might have been rails was only dew on ground-running tendrils reflecting the light of the moon, or reflecting the kiln-flames from the Valley itself.

Beneath vines, beneath wind-blown gorse, I sensed there were only very ancient rows of bricks which of their own weight and a thousand years of rain were sinking inexorably into the earth from whence they came.

Stupefied, I sat down on a low turtle-shaped mound of pottery shards—said nothing at all.

As in a moment of vision, all the things heretofore not known or taken on faith in all my life suddenly became clear. I understood. After this knowledge there was no forgiveness.

I looked up. I intended to share with her my revelation.

In her face I saw something both significant and terrible.

She sat erect, smiled. Her face was full of another kind of wonder, an expression I knew too well. Although she saw what I saw, her mind, her imagination, was different. She had never been on the high escarpments.

Therefore I understood she did in fact see "railroad yards." She saw what she had to see: docks, barges, and long lines of freight cars rolling. Her faith was absolute; she had never seen her own face burning like a rose inside a kiln.

Only because of me she had come here, because of love—and that was enough.

Perhaps we might have returned the way we came. With good fortune, I might have lived out life in the

kilns, an outcast because of my fatal knowledge, a tooth-
less, muttering grader of shards. Perhaps her spirit
really was the spirit of the cedar forests from which no
woman ever returned. Perhaps there was Justice after
all, in the pattern of our loin cloths.

But I did not turn back.

I pointed ahead to a low notch in a wall, and to the
dark canyon of stone beyond.

With impulsive almost childish glee, with her long,
black hair blowing in the first wind of morning, she
took my hand. She raised me to my feet.

She laughed and I laughed and as we ran the longest
journey of our life began.

The sun rose.

As we paused for the last time to look back, far away
and far below, I saw the high escarpments turn for one
moment into flame.

The path leading always upward took us between
flowers and across the first high-mountain meadow.
There in a grove of sweet, low-growing pines for the
first time, we made love and then slept in each other's
arms until the sun was overhead.

III

THE URBAN WARS

In the Eye of the Storm

Shall I keep ringing that number?

Their washer was gone. The hot and cold water hoses were melted gun barrels pointing at the utility room floor. In the kitchen their refrigerator had left an oblong of grey lint on the floor, but the mixer and juicer and electric knife sharpener remained on the Formica counter. Depford knew the installers and the men taking away other appliances had milled through the house, getting in each other's way.

And now his wife was also gone.

In the bedroom Depford found nothing at all: the night stand, her records, their waterbed, and the water cooler with Natural Spring Water were gone.

Now Depford could not remember exactly which items he had ordered sent from stores and which items he had traded back as down payments. This new disorder was complete, yet Depford believed he had it all recorded on sales slips in his pockets—a separate pocket in his clothes for each room in this re-echoing house, in the smoky night of their suburb, the steel mill lights of Gary, hanging in the night sky.

Depford imagined it well enough:

Louise was all right except when people came and took things away from their bedroom. Probably the bedroom people arrived to take everything just as the new things arrived. So Louise left. Again. Depford knew she had called a taxi, or to save them money she might have ridden to the YWCA in a furniture van.

So he sat in the corner of the bedroom and listened to the sand from the plaster grind between his coat and the bedroom walls as he moved his shoulders up and down, tried to sleep.

Before dawn rain began to fall across the bedroom windows. Outside Depford heard corrugated boxes pop and whisper beneath raindrops. Across the roofs of the suburb, towards Gary and Greater Chicago, angora tails of smoke rose from chimneys into low clouds.

After Depford was fully awake and had found a raincoat, he went outside into the first sleet.

Now a large pile of boxes and crates were astride the front walk: a half-dozen shipments had arrived during the night. The new, larger crates began also to pop and bulge.

Depford tried to bring all of the new shipments into their house. Then he remembered the tarpaulins in the cellar: once Depford had written ad copy about some fine tarpaulins, had bought six.

Then it was fully light, and Depford saw a great many more crates and smaller boxes, one labeled "Cabinet, Medicine."

The advertising agency would very soon expect him to arrive for work; Depford also had the premonition this time Willer might just fire him.

Therefore Depford stopped worrying about the crates astride the front walk and about Louise for he really wanted to shave and to get back to work after this latest buying spree. At that moment he understood what it must be like to be an alcoholic—as with buying things avidly, but unable to remember all of every transaction.

Depford wanted to shave, but a pick-up crew had repossessed his razor and his mirror when they took the old medicine cabinet off the bathroom wall. And was that yesterday, or during the night while he slept?

She wants the baby—doctors won't let her.

At the ad agency, Depford had his head on the desk when they fired him.

At two o'clock he had opened one eye, exactly at the moment someone slipped the final paycheck under his arm, very near his half-parted lips.

While Depford cleaned out his desk, the Copy Chief came in and slapped him on the back and said those old papers could wait. Said Mr. Willer wants very much to speak to you.

Willer was Vice-President. Could not understand all of this. What about all of this? Hated it, of course, but when there is no recourse then there is no recourse. Do you not agree, Dep, Old Sod?

Depford said he did agree. Depford supposed he should attend more to business instead of walking out to lunch with all the carbons of his own ad copy. Of course he did call back that one time and the Copy Chief had said . . .

"Cer-tain-ly," Mr. Willer broke in. "No areas of dis-agreement in your case need be defined, Dep Old Sod."

The Copy Chief sat on a stool in the corner.

At lunch Willer had stated he wanted to get to the bottom of this. So the Copy Chief wanted to listen.

"As I would see it, Dep Old Sod," Willer said, "what you need is a budget."

Mr. Willer began to draw lines on a piece of paper.

"Let's say you get a job: say, fifty thou? Suppose twenty percent goes to the shelter. Now then . . ."

Depford did not follow it.

Around their house there had been many budgets, some filled out for three consecutive weeks. Mr. Willer's budget reminded Depford of the sleet that came down like chips of porcelain, and still he had not found where Louise was hiding.

"Give away, to keep up with the down Jones," Mr. Willer seemed to be saying. "But remember: stanff cane. Ladenoff, and makes sense, huh?"

Yes, except the Copy Chief wanted to say a few words at this time. Copy agreed with Willer, but also wanted to point out—for the record—there was no request for stuff by Old Dep on new model cars. Old Dep had imagined that assignment; therefore had assigned that copy job to himself. Surely?

Copy Chief sat back on his stool.

Mr. Willer wanted to say a few words to back up what he had said.

While Willer and Copy Chief talked, Depford remembered how he had come here in the first place. In grade school each afternoon he read dictionaries, his hobby; he tried to find words like "gonad." In classes he heard what everyone said, and on tests he wrote what he heard; that was always enough. His adopted mother and father were both schoolteachers. Because they had no children they got little Depford from a local attorney. Depford thought this was true, but he did not believe all the circumstances were public knowledge. In high school he won a jingle contest and was summoned to this Agency to receive his prize, and to hear his entry set to music. For the second contest he submitted an entry that was still being played on radio stations in the

South. After that everyone said Depford should go into advertising.

After graduation Willer gave him a desk and a cubicle all his own.

After they were married nine months, Louise knew something was wrong. Professionally. Alone, she understood Depford must write ad copy directly from the product: had to write while staring at a bottle of Sweet-Mo or an illuminated plastic worm for night fishing.

Then Copy Chief found out. He said realism will take you far.

But Louise was the first to know how far sincerity would take Depford when a case of double-ended toothpicks were delivered to the door. That day in their basement she found other things Depford had written ad copy about and had then compulsively bought: tarpaulins; a blue, polished, felt-lined box of veterinarian tools. The day Willer assigned second-car copy, Depford brought home a second car.

"Whiskey I could understand," Louise said. "Or horses. Or maybe women. I could even understand gardening."

Then Depford wrote about and signed to purchase a folded-up, plastic wading pool, delivered in midwinter. For the first time, Louise left him: counseling was no good.

Mr. Willer stood.

Yes, Depford could go now, could go find Louise. Had this little session helped?

The Copy Chief thought it certainly had helped.

Everyone stood up and everyone shook hands and everyone said, "Good luck to you."

Depford knew the truth. He was what every advertisement agency assumed: the perfect customer, the man who believed. Except Depford was a more pure type than any

imagined customer for initially he had to believe to pro-
duce his copy; then he could not resist what he, himself,
had written. There was no disbelief in him. He was paid
for sincerity, but he was known as a fool. Because he was
innocent, all that was kept from him.

Consequently he was very much in debt to every
client of Willer's agency because everything he bought
was on credit.

Now Depford could go find his wife.

First, however, Depford checked their home. Louise
was still absent, had not slipped back during the day,
really had gone to morning and afternoon and night
movies.

Now the crates from his last shipments were gone.

The tarps were folded and stacked. Everything that
had been outside was now installed or nailed up or
tacked down. Her new kitchen was a four-color spread.
Had they really forwarded his message to her room at
the YWCA?

Behind the house, Depford saw empty crates and
boxes and excelsior piled higher than the roof. The
neighbors would complain next spring when they saw
the first rat.

In the center of the newly carpeted, newly furnished
living room floor, sleep took him.

Depford had been awake nearly two days. Without
thinking anything at all he felt himself spreading out, all
parts of his body bearing an equal weight in the center
of a new carpet. He buttoned his coat around his neck
and breathed deeply, much like a stonemason's apprentice breathes deeply on a pile of old cement bags at
noon after his first morning's work.

The telephone rang. It was Louise.

Louise was calling from the YWCA.

Louise had an idea.

Keep Smiling: there is no time like the pleasant.

Before Depford could turn off the motor, or could doze off to sleep, Louise ran down the steps of the YWCA and got in on the driver's side of their car. Very much Depford was now awake.

Louise said she could not sleep at the YWCA. Knew she ought to be more brave and more understanding. Knew she would never leave again. Kissed Depford very tenderly.

Depford said it was all right. Now everything was installed and their new kitchen was a real four-color spread dream.

About idea: Louise said her idea came from the TV at the YWCA. Had heard a message: could they Consolidate?

Must arrive at Consolidate before ten o'clock. After Louise parked their car in front of the loan building she had to wake Depford once more.

Mr. Lookey was in. Pronounced "Lucky" he said. Offered them cigars, and two packs of gum. "Problem you got; problem we . . . now what is this all about anyhow?"

Louise began with how they met. She had been traveling through this small town. There was a street fair. A man had put them in the same seat of "The Bug." They fell in love . . . Then Louise came to the part about the Agency, and how he had to work all the time. Of course she liked to work at the Agency too because they could have the things they ought to have. Finally she told Mr. Lookey about the Copy Chief.

The Copy Chief had given the House Beautiful copy to Depford on purpose, a kind of office joke. So Depford wrote this beautiful ad copy.

Mr. Lookey said, "Yes, indeed. Only young once. Now let's proceed."

He got out a pad of paper and drew some lines on it.
"Young fellow," he said, "you wake up here and give
me the answers."

And then to her, "The mangement of money is the
key to happiness."

Mr. Lookey asked how much would they make if the
two of them kept right on working at some other
Agency, here at the peak of prosperity? And how much,
since prosperity was going to get more so, together
would they make in twenty-one years? Finally Mr.
Lookey ripped off the page from his scratch pad. "Makes
sense, does it not?"

Louise said it did. Mr. Lookey said, "Yus, does."

Outside the neon sign flashed back through the window, "etadilosnoC, etadisosnoC."

Beyond the glass brick window and the planting of
dwarf evergreens, they saw trolley-bus cables intersect
in exact squares against the sky. Rain came down into
the street once more, pecked at the glass brick window.
Somewhere among the geraniums, inside, a transformer
for the Consolidate-neon hummed like a winter bug in
the first hour of hibernation.

Mr. Lookey said, "We buy payments. That's business. You then pay my firm a lump sum each month.
Pay one instead of many little litt-le payments. We don't
care if you two have jobs or not. You are Youth, and
wide-open, U.S. double A. That's our security. Is it
not?"

Mr. Lookey said he wanted them to have cash. He
signed the papers after they signed. He went to the safe,
and the door swung open very easily.

Louise and Depford got back in the car once more.
Depford felt better, and so did Louise. Before she could
drive away, however, Mr. Lookey had closed the loan

office. It was almost midnight, but Mr. Lookey nevertheless was standing on the curb, tapping on the window of their car.

"Only young once," he said. "Have a good day!"

Because it was late and because Depford had been
going nearly three days, they decided on a motel. They
would drive out to the bungalow tomorrow afternoon,
when tomorrow came.

For professional services: well visit. Remit, please.

When they again opened their eyes the snow was in
drifts outside the motel windows. Depford telephoned
for sandwiches. Everything was so warm they stayed
another day, listened to the television game shows, won-
dered when the snow would cease to fall. They missed
her records and the water cooler, but they talked over
everything several times. Finally when Depford had
dozed one more day, he awakened, and got up, and
began to walk up and down the room of their motel
unit. Time to leave.

On the way home, on top of the last rise of ground,
they parked for a minute to look down upon the suburb:
one house was an igloo held in the jawbone of a frozen
river.

She asked, why the igloo?

Depford said, "It's the crates. In our back yard."

As the sun lowered itself into a cloud bank, Depford
drove on down the hill, allowed their car to feel its way
through the drifts of evening.

Inside the bungalow they found nothing at all.

Everything, every single thing, was gone. Again.

Louise began to cry.

She went up to the bare walls. She touched them with
the ends of her long fingers. She ran into the bedroom.

By accident, the people repossessing things had forgotten their bed. She threw herself on their waterbed and pulled her knees up very close to her chin.

Depford also walked through all the rooms. He could hear her sobbing a little.

Depford wandered into the utility room. The hose from their old automatic washer was still a melted gun barrel, still aimed at the floor. In the center of the utility room was a scarlet outboard motor. He could not remember writing that copy. Perhaps the Copy Chief had played another little joke.

Everything in the four-color spread kitchen that had been newly installed before Louise called from the YWCA was gone: the knife sharpener, the toaster, the juicer, the grater, the slicer. Only a red plaid clock hung on the kitchen wall. Depford plugged in the cord and stood for two minutes watching the scarlet second hand go around and around.

In the bedroom Louise was trying to put clean sheets on the waterbed.

Depford tried to put his arm around her, but she twisted away. She did not want to be touched—not ever touched—by anyone. After the bed was made, Louise got in without taking off her shoes.

Depford sat in the corner a long time.

While they were two days at the motel, the vans no doubt came back. A van must have appeared out of the dark and backed up to the front door. By now everything he had bought on his last big shopping tour was buried in a warehouse near the river, with other lots of used furniture and unclaimed freight and scrap metal from crashed airplanes.

Something like that, or was this all a mistake? Perhaps someone forgot to write "thirty days" in a blank;

perhaps one blank in all those papers was never filled out in the first place. . . .

Near midnight Louise smelled smoke.

Somewhere against the wall, where his face was, she saw his cigarette burning.

Louise got out of bed and came over to him and took his hands. She sat on the floor beside him and kissed him very tenderly. Louise said it was all right. It was no mistake of his. It was her idea to Consolidate everything. She, herself, had heard the message on TV.

She said, finally, it was that Mr. Lookey.

Depford had known it all along.

No Deposits, No Returns.

At noon the auctioneers sold everything Depford had dredged up from their basement "reserves": the tarpaulins, the veterinarian's tools, the double-ended toothpicks. In fact the outboard motor went for much more than half of what it cost, for the crate was not damaged.

When Depford returned home and plugged in a new little radio, and when the music came on, Louise felt much better. Louise opened two cans and put the soup on a two-burner hot plate. Very good, for stored away in their own basement were at least two more automobile loads of soup and other things and they could live out of their own basement—almost like savings—until spring or even into early summer.

Together they sat on the waterbed; ate soup from cans.

Depford said absolutely everything they really needed was within easy reach: the new hot plate, the radio. They could block off the rest of the house; they would not see or feel the empty rooms. In fact, she said their bedroom was much like a good motel unit, except they had cooking privileges. Beyond the windowpanes lay bright, leveling snow.

Depford said the two of them, alone in the bedroom, were in some kind of pure state, like the snow, as though they unconsciously had been seeking just that. What they had purchased was gone; what they owned was Consolidated. What had been repossessed by the vans had gone for interest in advance, and all the carrying charges; consequently what they now owed was for the things he bought on the way home the day they fired him.

Louise did not understand exactly, but she said they would now live within their means, and this was something like a budget.

After lunch they lay side by side on the waterbed. They talked about jobs, and how Mr. Willer would soon eat lunch again with the Copy Chief. The Copy Chief would call on the telephone and say, "obligation," say "old time's sake," and so on.

They were considering what should be said in return when their doorbell rang.

Before it rang again, Depford ran upstairs to hide.

Louise answered the door.

At the curb she saw two blue coupés, parked, their motors feeding. The coupés were parked side by side, as though they traveled in pairs. The two drivers had walked side by side to the door of their bungalow.

The two men wore identical pearl-grey Homburgs and black coats with pearl-grey felt on the collars. They looked so much alike that she was surprised to see two sets of footprints leading to the front steps.

The man who was left-handed took off his Homburg. His hair was grey, with streaks of black near the roots, much like a woman's hair after she has fixed herself up to work when the ad suggests applicants be "dignified."

Before either of the men had a chance to speak, Louise said to them very firmly through her crack in the door:

"Nothing wrong here."

The man who had rung the doorbell was also the most agile. He stepped forward and put his face very close to the crack in the door.

He smiled.

"I'm from Mr. Lookey. Mr. Lookey says give you best regards. Mr. Lookey says, 'Have a good one.'"

Then the man who was left-handed, and who had rung the doorbell, put his hat back on his grey hair and turned and walked briskly to his coupé and drove away, still smiling a lucky smile.

The other man in an identical pearl-grey Homburg sidled close enough to hear it all. He was a listener. He was not a talker. Someone in the home office had unreasonably or mistakenly sent both men on another useless errand. Always they were sent to the same addresses, but they were never allowed to work together. Of course, except at banquets, they never spoke.

"Business," he told Louise. "With a Mr. Depford."

"Not here," she said, as though to drive the man away. "Out of town!"

The man stepped back another step. Deliberately he looked at their upstairs windows.

Behind a dormer, he saw Depford's face. He pointed his finger towards the window and said, "Ah, ha!" He kicked at his own footprints in the snow. He pointed a rolled-up envelope at Depford's face behind the windows.

Then the man stood beside his dented blue coupé. He turned once more to fix the location of this house exactly in his mind.

He was very interested in their bedroom. He had the look of someone who might come back very soon, probably after dark. He stamped his foot in the snow and waved at the dormer window and said something to the snow.

Without hesitation he got into the car, and without sliding or spinning a wheel, he followed the track of the other car and like an apparition vanished around the corner.

Depford and Louise ran outside.

What the man in the coupé said to the snow seemed to hover close to the frozen ground; his threat or his message remained frozen, suspended in the motionless air of their yard. What the words might be they could not say: "See you in church," or, "See you in court," or, "See you, see you, see you."

They faced each other in the cold air and they listened very carefully but their ears could not know.

Together they walked back into the house.

Depford sat once more in the corner with the sand from the plaster rubbing into his shoulder. Louise felt like going to bed, but she stopped at the packing box chifforobe to see if there was any music on the radio.

Some music would do them both good.

Besides the sun had not yet even begun to set.

Beirut

From his fifth-floor apartment with the usual balcony and parapet and a low railing for safety about neck high, his view was framed by other apartment walls with balconies, all looking down to an intersection of two streets.

Noon, the sidewalks motionless: the apartment canyons reverberated from diesel truck traffic on other streets and also from small-arms fire, restless, as though for practice being fired at the sun.

Because he had lived in this apartment longer than one month, he knew the intersection below, towards nightfall, might become something like outdoor theatre, or burning-automobile theatre. At noon, however, all Moslem or Christian or Counter-counter Revolutionaries apparently slept.

Even so the Correspondent avoided all low-rent balconies and in fact only camped at this place. The prior tenants, Turks, had left everything.

The French television correspondent had arrived and said in English, "With ice, please," and now both the American Correspondent and the French television person drank from heavy, glass, blue telephone-crossarm insulators. Their vermouth, apparently, was from Algeria.

The Frenchman's English was a little broken, but so was his German and about six words of Arabic. The American did only English, so in Beirut he was careful and did not expect just yet to be killed. The Correspondent was, however, killed much later but in a different city.

"Warm," the French television correspondent said, hesitated, then relied on what he read in newspapers, "a warm, human interest story. For heart strings."

"Moreover," and the American Correspondent squeezed a lemon into his blue insulator glass, "she is regular. You see her twenty past four. Daily."

The television correspondent who put everything on TV tapes and air mailed his tapes direct to Zurich repeated 16:20 hours in French.

"As I said at the Club: you view it, you like it, it's yours. I can't use it. From my balcony get your camera angle; the shit in the gutters gives you real-life Beirut. The burned-out taxi cab gives you war-torn Beirut . . ."

The American waited to see if the French television man got it all right, did not think so.

"I mean every day. Regardless. I've seen automatic weapon fire and grenades coming down from balconies. Not safe for any mortal. But she appears. Understand?"

"Perfectly. Maybe eight, maybe ten years old. No?"

"Yes," the American Correspondent finished his vermouth, nodded. "Certified."

"Dressed, you say? In white?"

"White dress. Also a head covering or white scarf. A little girl in a white dress."

To himself, in French, the television correspondent said, "White-dress girl walks through gunfire" and saw it as right for all television screens. He, himself, would add the necessary element of mystery.

In English he asked the American: this white-dress girl. Mission unknown. Background unknown. Her psychology, the reason for her existence unknown?

The American Correspondent nodded, yes.

"But: In war-torn Beirut, no one shoot her. Elect not to kill a young girl. Who just strolling?"

"I know nothing about her family, or sect, or whatever."

"Ralph, not necessary. We *know* what she does: walks."

"For sure: diagonal. At the intersection. Never runs. Never hesitates. Charmed life."

"Ahhh," and the French correspondent saw his story angle, "our charmed-life girl."

"Also returns. Same route. Sometimes with a sack. Once I saw a chicken head dangling from a bag."

The French television correspondent liked it: to obtain food in war-torn Beirut a girl in white braves often automatic-weapon fire.

At four o'clock, they stood on the balcony.

Much nearer now, they heard the *thuck-thuck-thuck* of small-arms fire; twice mortar shells landed in an alley between white, masonry walls. About now, every afternoon, the shelling began.

Below the balcony, all around the intersection, the iron shutters of what were sometimes store fronts rolled down by themselves, eyes closing.

"As stated," the American Correspondent said and at the balcony parapet, side by side, they looked down.

The girl was on the sidewalk, then at the curb, a white dress against a steel-shuttered door.

Very much as children are taught, this one looked carefully both directions. As though putting her toe in hot water, she stepped down from the curb and as though balancing on an invisible tight-wire walked diagonally across the street, walked without haste, walked towards the stutter of gunfire. Disappeared.

Into what door or window or gate or passageway, they could not say.

Nothing happened for some minutes, but the French correspondent with strong connections in Zurich saw deeper into it.

"We witness the bravery of innocence: mystery girl obtains family foods in war-torn Lebanon. Dateline, Beirut."

"As stated," for now she was coming back, a shadow of white against rolled-down shutters. Again she looked obediently in both directions for traffic, did not break or run when bricks from a rooftop crashed behind her into the street.

"Hey, she scored bread."

The young girl in white now carried two loaves of French bread though there were no known bread stores in this vicinity.

The French television correspondent had seen what he came to see and therefore in English said, "Many thanks, Ralph. You are very helpful to me. Yes, many thanks, Ralph."

Also: these contrast, the setting, these human, delicate aspect absolutely suited to our media. Yes: bring home the human side of war-torn Beirut. For which, Ralph, I scoop. No?

That's why the French television person out of Zurich returned the next day, a Tuesday.

This time he set up two cameras behind the balcony railing. One camera had its own power-pack. One had a long, black telephoto lens.

Exactly on schedule, the girl in white appeared: same

place, except now the gunfire was very close, and at least two mortar bursts, one phosphorus.

The French television man pointed his cameras from the balcony rail down the street.

While the American was in the kitchen getting more ice, he heard one camera explode. Shatter.

He ran back to the balcony, insulator-glass in hand.

The French person was down.

Half on the balcony, half inside the living room. Hit.

One bullet had entered the neck. Had ripped off a quadrant of the jaw. Severed the big neck artery. Also veins.

Ralph packed towels first around the neck. Then more towels. Then the sheets from the bed. Anything.

Blood kept pumping out. Although he could not speak or breathe, the French person understood pretty well what was happening for he kept shaking his head, "No. No. No . . ."

After the Frenchman died, blood continued to spread because the towels and sheets and everything were soaked.

After the American Correspondent moved out the next day to another apartment and then moved again, he thought somewhat less about it. Even so, several times at the Club, either drinking or not, he concluded, always, by saying it had to be one of two ways:

Possibly that guy's cameras *resembled* gun barrels pointing down from the balcony. So a sniper did it, because they also everyday watched the girl in white.

Or secondly, a thing the correspondent did not wholly believe:

They sent a young recruit, a different boy each day at the scheduled hour, dressed as a girl, perhaps to do movement-training. Or possibly to cause someone—as with a camera set-up on a balcony—to expose *themselves* and that way to train a more experienced, older recruit to use urban terrains productively.

But probably the first: a sniper made a mistake.

In either event, about ten days later at the Club in a much better part of Beirut, the Correspondent met the French person's replacement.

A real Swiss. From Zurich. Direct.

A Rumor of Metal

After nineteen years in this frightful climate, I remained
extraordinarily healthy. Moreover I understood our
Territorial Police mission in the midcontinent river
basins. As I rose in rank from Constable to OC/OMT, I
ran things by the Manual (as revised). Mine is a large
territory; I know each creek. I shave every day and do
not like people who make their own little rules.

No matter: towards the end of the winter rains I was
reviewing my Ops Reports of past years. Our Secure-
Base people on the Gulf know only what someone dis-
patches down-river. My replacement was due any week
and therefore I was reviewing *all* files—a conscientious
thing to do.

At the time of that up-river incident—what, ten years
ago?—the two boys were about nine years of age—and
one had red hair. Even over the intervening years,
vividly, I remember the red hair.

In re-reading my Ops report, I saw no harm in it—
and nothing could ever be proved. Oh, possibly at the
time my relationship with that Town-Major was a little

bit special—nothing more. At two o'clock in the morning, rain coiled and struck the wall and ran like a many-legged animal across the shutter.

With that file in hand, I recalled everything—and especially the boy with the red hair.

To be entirely candid, the moment of recall was also poignant: having been in the Old Mississippi Territory for so many years, and as yet not officially detailed to a Secure-Base on the Gulf, I was a father to no one. I felt very much alone, even bereft, for in my hand I held the future of two boys.

II

That morning a renegade american came down-river to sell news. Astride his log, he had paddled two nights. Towards dawn he had rolled his log on to the mud flat below my Headquarter's landing. In the lee of his paddle-log, the american slept on the mud until the sun rose higher in the sky. Eventually he got up, scratched himself, and walked the slope towards my Headquarters: a verified cooperator, from a bluffs settlement, more than a day's go up-river on a tertiary stream.

I always keep informants waiting: it helps them organize their story.

Then for an hour I worked the american. My verified's execrable, broken speech was frontier hyperbole and lies. Nothing any of them *ever* says is either direct or descriptive; after so many generations their argot of defeat became the accepted language of a continent.

The more I listened to the verified, the more I understood he was reporting—possibly—some real metal. Moreover, he claimed this metal was "fabricated." But was his *story* fabricated? Or was this alleged metal "fabricated"? They always say "fabricated": It is their national obsession. *Osthot?*

In reply, the verified said one of two things: either this find was as big as a mountain; or, this big metal was inside a mountain. Something like that.

Rumor or fact, I was going up-river. If metal were reported, I would take immediate, appropriate action—and possibly pick up an extra levy of work-age males. I *know* they are not able to use metal, but field officers up-river also understand they secretly continue to "experiment," as though by merely "natural" procedures they might again fabricate something. Just suppose, against all odds, a non-verified found a process to use metal: wouldn't that be an actionable development? Wouldn't that thing spread, like some fatal, clandestine disease?

That's why a metal find, a cache, or even the rumor of metal is one thing never ignored in my Territory.

I called for my flat-bottom, the twelve-oar skiff.

My work is essentially river work. To follow even the rumor of metal I will go to the farthest reach of any tributary until my coaster-boat or skiff grounds on mud in one inch of water. Very much I value the oarsmen.

I was already dressed for patrol, was waiting at day-break on the landing, when I saw my best crew emerge from their barrack/boathouse. Six men on each side, they moved their legs in unison: a machine, a twelve-legged, running animal carrying my skiff. They launched, then leaped to their stations, almost as one person. Across each crew-member's back was a Go-bag: with their Go-bags of food they often live for one week aboard a skiff and through the daylight hours row steadily.

This particular crew pleased me. Any crew-chief,

naturally, is a verified; this one was a small Black man, with a resonant, rowing, coxswain voice. Many a day in rain or nearly adrift, partly lost in the green fogs, we had worked the river and the creeks. He drove the oarsmen; I called the course and speed. He did his work; I did mine. We use americans to row.

Then it was noon on the sunlit water, the Coxswain driving the oarsmen, their backs two lines of sweat-covered, precision sculpture in motion. Each year after the rains the channels are utterly changed. There is no vegetation for miles beyond the serrated river banks, but in spring always I see a washed, dynamic beauty in the knobs of clay which stretch inland towards a mirage of blue, motionless smoke. This horizon-line marks the escarpments where shrubs first put down roots in granite. The day was cloudless, and the Black Coxswain's chanting voice at times seemed to echo down upon us from the sky.

To observe more closely another kind of change, I pointed my skiff through a break in what once was a levee of the east bank. Here the water sprawls inland across many square miles of barely navigable sloughs. These sloughs once were fertile valleys where rivers joined and flowed south to the gulf. And here, also, lay their cities: sunk like outmoded, ill-designed vessels of war, long ago covered by silt.

During the last rains, by chance, this channel had become almost straight; the skiff moved easily on ten feet of clear water across what once had been the edge of a town—a small one, a place now nameless, with not even a Survey Number on our charts.

Beneath the skiff's bottom the water unexpectedly became more shallow. To find deeper water, the Coxswain steered abruptly left between two clay humps. Ahead and below, lay the "mainstreet" of this town, its "roofs" a few feet beneath our boat.

The oarsmen pulled twice, then shipped the oars. We drifted without a sound, as though we were strolling, in springtime, along the sidewalks of another age.

Never had I seen the facade of a town so precisely outlined: the current had swept the gutters clean; in store fronts the display windows still faced the street. One window display, anchored in light silt, was nearly complete: a child's three-wheeled, wooden toy, with the carved head of a horse; a square, picket-side crib for a baby; terra-cotta heads of dolls, all in a row, their eyes now vacant holes; yes, and three wooden, toy guns, still pointed at the running water of the street. In two weeks, on the surface, the summer algae would grow again. This street, accidentally exposed, would be cut off again from the sunlight by a foot of ochre-colored scum.

We are not interested in their archeology so I do not know the circumstance which preserved a facade in this way. As their metal softened and gave way—a thing which hastened the war's end—all their buildings gradually collapsed. Perhaps in the final war days this city was sunk by us at the identical time their metal was giving way; whereupon encroaching mud propped up everything along these two city blocks. Future spring floods will destroy even this temporary, delicate balance.

My oarsmen looked down into this street where once their forebears walked and lived. To my oarsmen the facade was without meaning, was only a shimmering apparition, a thing if either exposed to air or touched by swimmers would collapse in whole sections. As we drifted, the oarsmen did not change expression. They were grateful for this suspended moment of calm, their oars shipped.

By indirection, by other channels, we found the main course of the river. Again the Coxswain's voice drove the oars.

Towards noon the next day I saw the first bank-side watchtowers. Then we rowed more slowly, more publicly; first up the tributary, and then steadily between narrow banks of clay.

At the end of a shallow creek, I saw the cliff-face of red earth, the landmark from which the settlement takes its name, "Ochretown."

The rumor of metal had brought me here.

III

Seen from the landing, their town lay motionless beneath its own smoke, a curved, brown river-slug of clay houses. The walls and the roofs of fired-clay shards rose in random tiers between the creek bank and the base of the ochre cliff. Higher, across the cliff-face, I saw their second town: dark, square room-holes, connected by tunnels. In flood time the town moves up the cliff-face and lives miserably until the waters recede.

–You *see* gun?

My counterpart up-river, my Town-Major, had followed me respectfully from the landing to his "Headquarters," and now we were alone in his connected rooms, the walls of pounded earth, one floor covered with muddy rushes. The Town-Major's "desk" was a valuable piece of wood, squared on four sides as though by industrial process, placed trestle-like across fired-clay pedestals. To me the desk symbolized their pathetic reliance on meaningless form; to him, doubtless, the "desk" was a psychic necessity, a holdover from a past when real furniture apparently signified industrial power.

I nodded, Yes. Before starting up-river I had seen gun. Very close in fact *seen*.

–*Osthot?* and my Town-Major leaned across his "desk." Might you have *him*. Now?

To be effective in the Territories, you must understand their *minds*. My Town-Major's enquiry was in part ritualistic, as when more sensitive people make enquiries about personal health, or the weather. For example, "Is *it* happy" or "Is Little Friend asleep?" to them means, "Has the gun lately been discharged? cleaned? oiled? etc." Normally, a Town-Major will not expect each visit to see my gun. With all my counterparts, however, I hold out the possibility of the direct, visual experience.

"Little Friend is *very* near," I said. "He will be happy—sometime—to see light."

–*Osthot?* and my Town-Major placed his hands palm down on the narrow top of his desk, as though to hold on. In many ways he was an able man, but the possibility of seeing it, close-up, caused a visible, almost unbearable, vaguely sexual, tension in his whole body. For all americans there is magic in it; therefore I use their primitive belief for their own self-governance. I now had him ready for business.

"Metal contact, Town-Major. Reported."

–I reported it, Commissioner.

At precisely such moments great administrative restraint with americans is required. I saw two possibilities: the verified on the log in fact was the Town-Major's courier, but profit being the ideological fury of their lives, the man riding the log had assumed the role of informer. Or, when I rowed past the watchtowers, my

Town-Major concluded there was a rumor of metal in his enclave.

Effectiveness in the Territories, however, means one is never diverted by *anything* they say. If I had paid an official courier, it was only a cost of governance; if the two men later shared my nominal fee paid unnecessarily, I could admire their tact. All of that I understood, and I do not like it very much for I go by the Manual (as revised):

"You interrogated? Under Section 4?"

From an otherwise able man I got only hyperbole, their eye-rolling "anguish." At the close of a three-minute evasion, I heard the word "Sincere." Always they end lies by "sincere" for it is their signal-word for, "Negative, No."

"I appreciate," and the irony always eludes them, "your sincerity. Therefore we have work. You and I."

My Town-Major was clearly relieved. Instead of taking a prescribed action, he had called me, by courier, up-river. When he said "sincere," I understood absolutely there was found metal, somewhere.

I stood. Using their own gesture for "action," I slapped my thigh: "Go."

The Town-Major was out the door ahead of me, leading the way.

Above all they like action, but they seldom calculate ultimate consequence; to them the going is more important than any policy.

With the Town-Major ahead, with one-half my crew following, we went at a half-trot to the town's edge, then skirted the ochre cliff; by ever-more narrow paths to the north and west, across terrain of rock-face and clay knob, we walked more steeply towards the sun.

Where we went was once a valley. Ahead, stone outcrop marked the ancient ridgeline. Knobs of clay, at this place transformed by wind into grotesque, guardian figures, showed traces of mineral; in crevasses which might trap water the first purple lichens grew.

My Town-Major stopped. He signalled the rowers. They sat down beside the path to wait, their heads at rest on their unslung Go-bags.

At the next rise, the trail abruptly stopped.

Below my feet I saw an amphitheatre, a whirlpool shape of stone two hundred yards across, its walls in past winters scoured by tornado-like winds, falling away—down, down—to the valley floor. What at first seemed empty seat-rows, aisles, and exits were only illusions: sunlight falling across slabs of stone. The Town-Major again pointed to the bottom, the north face.

On stilts, in white relief against granite, I saw an intact section of a poured-concrete freeway. These monumental shards, up-ended in sand, are not unusual; this section, however, was fifty yards long, a black stripe down the centre, an elevated "bridge" leading to and from nowhere. Once a highway of importance ran along the valley floor to one of their cities now gone.

The Town-Major started down the rock-face, and I followed.

Finally, at the bottom, my Town-Major stopped. Breathing heavily, perspiring, he leaned with one hand on the smooth, white stilt of the old freeway. We both looked back and up to the rim of the amphitheatre and into the cloudless sky beyond.

–This place, and the Town-Major slapped his thigh. Here they play the game.

I said nothing.

Abruptly the Town-Major turned to the ladder-steps of the concrete stilt and began to climb.

Below him, following carefully, I also climbed.

–*Yako*, Commissioner?

I had patrolled the guardrails of this elevated ruin, kicking debris as I went. The men who discovered this anomaly of wind and stone had returned often to play. The black centre-stripe had become one baseline; stone shards, once almost round, lay everywhere and I saw broken, sun-dried balls of clay. With perhaps nine players of the game on each side, they threw or rolled balls with great force towards improvised, stone "houses"; if a ball went cleanly through a little house, all players of the game could change base, could Go. This elevated "court" was absolutely level, absolutely smooth, a perfect place: I imagined voices of men re-echoing up and across the stone amphitheatre's rim.

–*Yako?*

I *yakoed* enough: here was artifact discovery (not reported and here was artifact usage [casual]). The rumor of metal had nothing to do with it.

My Town-Major looked away, said nothing.

I expected no answer for every Field Officer and every Town-Major have their little trade-offs, the Manual (as revised) notwithstanding. We both understood playing a game constituted neither recovery of industrial process nor intent to reconstruct. Moreover, next season, the winds might again fill this amphitheatre with blown dust. Nevertheless, in one way, I was annoyed: had my trusted TM and a down-river courier cleverly worked me to buy *this* information? The news of play? No matter, I saw possible leverage in their little exercise: I might possibly extract a half-levy of men from Ochretown to train as oarsmen.

As though reading my thoughts, the Town-Major said, –Boys, only. Boys play here.

"*Osthot?*"

–Two boys. Also look. For good ones.

The Town-Major was at the railing. He pointed to

narrow pathways along the cliff-face. I understood two players of the game had gone farther and farther up and across the cliff-face looking for "balls."

Because of that, I, too, went into the tunnel of the mine.

As the two boys had come upon an entrance which blended absolutely with a crevasse in the face of the cliff, so did my Town-Major. Climbing up and along the cliff-face, only two steps ahead, my TM seemed to disappear into a shadow. One step more and I, too, was inside: a tunnel, cut with great precision through solid granite. Cool but not dank, wide enough for two, the tunnel led us a quarter of a mile through the steady dark.

As we walked, I thought of my oarsmen now probably asleep in the sun; without them I felt vulnerable for I was up-country, miles from my Headquarters; in the Territory, little tricks up-country are not unknown. Yet even in the dark, I had absolute confidence—and also the gun, the Little Friend.

Abruptly our mine shaft ended: we stood in the centre of a vaulted, half-lighted room, a place where four tunnels joined.

The Town-Major clapped his hands.

Sharply the sounds reverberated overhead, then ran away as though on noisy footsteps along the secondary corridors of what once had been one of their mines, possibly for coal.

On the floor of this vault, I saw two parallel ridges of rust: disintegrated rails which led to a larger drift, then probably fell away in a mile of darkness to the wall of silt which blocked an entrance where once men from the old valley assembled to work.

"Two Boys? Here?" and I imagined first their initial fright and then the reverberation of their echoes at search for stones.

–Only two, Commissioner. I have them.

"In regular? In Ochretown?"

–In Special custody.

Special meant the two were isolated-holds, not in the TM's regular cave. In the dark, when he could not see my face well, the Town-Major spoke without evasion: an able man, the kind of verified upon which my Territory depends. If Special-holds, were the boys also kin? Members of an elaborate "family" upon which his own authority in part rested? I cut through all of that:

"*Where* metal?"

Even though he was an american, Town-Major did not lie:

–Here, Commissioner.

By law the TM could not touch it, but I could touch it, and I did so by kicking.

Fifty yards back along a steeply rising, secondary tunnel, I walked around and around an ugly, low cart. The frame was metal; the corners bolted. The wheels were cast-metal, the rims flanged, the axles machined; front and rear was a hitch; there was a hand-wheel of metal, with a ratchet and cog which once had set the brakes. This find of metal to me was an ugly, repulsive thing. The cart shuddered and rocked in its own rust as I kicked, and kicked, and kicked.

Cars exactly like this, coupled all in a row, once hauled ore or coal to the mine's entrance in the valley. This thing, this rusted scab of their industry, had survived the most successful phase of that long-ago war when the weaponry of my forebears gradually de-tempered all their metal; moreover, this thing had survived all phases of the Metal-Purge Treaties at our war's end. Yet here it was, rotting but whole, disclosed by the play of boys in our own time. Rumors of metal brought me here, and now I had found it: sullen, hibernating in the fetid darkness of a cave.

"How many more? These things?"

–No more—now. You *yako*, Commissioner?

My Town-Major was pointing to the round stones which blocked the two, front, flanged wheels of the mine cart.

"No *yako*."

–Once five, he said patiently. Now *this* one, Commissioner.

I did not like it. One cart to be pulled from a mine, then raised above the amphitheatre walls, then hauled to Ochretown; there, after dark, this thing to be packed in mud, dried, then rafted down-river to a Gulf Base. The terms of the ancient Metal-Purge Treaties hang on.

Worse, the presence of metal made them restless. Even if the packing in mud were done in the Town-Major's restricted enclaves at night, there were always rumors. The americans catch the presence of metal as if catching a disease; soon the metal-disease becomes an epidemic of unrest. Depend on it: secretly they fear it but to touch or to hold metal is their obsession.

–Commissioner: you stand.

My Town-Major motioned me back to the place where the tunnels joined.

In the vaulted room I stood alone. The Town-Major's voice first seemed to whisper. Then his voice rolled along the tunnel from the place in darkness where the cart was:

–*Yako! Ya- K-O!* their word which means both to understand and to beware.

Like some low-runner, mindless animal the mine cart rattled in the tunnel; it gained speed, a thing long asleep now awakened.

Then it filled the low tunnel mouth, came out growing larger, an apparition of lunging metal.

Its front wheels hit two stones. Up the cart leaped, rose slowly, seemed for a moment to float like some hissing, wingless reptile. Half-turning, suspended in shadows above my head, it tilted forward, hit on the front trucks, bounced, skidded on a gash of sparks across stone, then end-over-end, disappeared like some wounded, rattling animal into the main shaft, going down.

In darkness it fell end-over-end, the cart shedding wheels, frames, trucks, bouncing on granite until it died against the mine's blocked entrance of silt.

In the silence, I heard one wheel, or one coupling, or a hand-brake rod bounce once, twice along a corridor of granite, and then everything was still. The air of the vault once more became very quiet, as water in a stretch of river becomes quiet after a stone sinks into the mud.

–Now you *yako*, Commissioner?

The cart overhead turning in its heavy parabola of flight left me dazed. By saying nothing at all, however, I gave my tacit approval: it was metal gone, and caves bear no witness.

–Rowers. Now we wake them?

I said, "Yes. Back to rowers. Go back Ochretown."

IV

In spring in my Territory the days are long. When we came back through the town's mudwall gates the sun overhead was halfway towards evening.

My rowers dropped off at the skiff where the other half of my crew was on either side of the up-turned hull putting Go-wax on the planks: their wax makes a "hot" skiff, one more easy to row.

While we had walked back from the cliff and the amphitheatre's rim and now for half an hour in the Town-Major's rooms, his "desk" between us, my TM explained away everything he had not yet done: Their little game on the freeway ruin was nothing? Agreed. Their search for round stones—not authorized— also was nothing? Agreed. Then two boys found carts coupled all in a row, in a tunnel; not knowing, not ever before having seen cast-metal or flanged wheels or spokes, not ever before having seen hand-wheel brakes or bolts holding two frames, why naturally these things they *no* understand, you *yako*, Commissioner?

Agreed, and now of course the last cart was gone and something like this could never again happen. But I knew the two boys *did* understand. When first they walked around the abandoned carts those things most certainly spoke to them. Embedded in the boy's language, in their legends, in their Myths of Power, of days when water became fire through whirling, dervish-Gods named *Torbeings*, without willing it so, two boys found in wheels and fabricated metal a confirmation of ancient, tribal dreams. Without having to understand they *knew* all carts Go.

Either by intent or by lack of enforcement they had touched metal; first the couplings, then a hand-wheel brake; then they probably sat in the carts, as though rowing a boat. Then one day they uncoupled a cart, pushed it a little; the wheels resting on granite turned, moved forward very easily. After the first cart lunged out of its tunnel, after it disappeared in a long, industrial gash of sparks, the boys were marked.

After two, after four carts went shrieking away, when

only one cart remained, the boys became frightened. At night, at bedtime, they confided to their mothers. Very well I understood: for two boys it was a religious experience, a conversion by metal.

"What action, Town-Major? What *action* you take?"

Suddenly my TM seemed older. I understood: with full-grown men he could have acted under Section 4 (as revised). Down-river my Hearings are absolutely correct, and my Court is Just—or at least no one has ever appealed. Moreover, I understood two boys were valuable, were the hope, were the future of fifty washed-away places like Ochretown. All Town-Majors rule by Theocratic force; their best hope for the town, for the race, is with the young. To invent games, to explore the darkness of tunnels showed early promise; these things I really did understand.

My Town-Major stood.

I followed through corridors. Being of mud and tile, Ochretown had its passages, warrens, stairs, and further passages. All these led upward. I knew the Special holds were in a carved-out room in the other city of the cliff's face, above all flood marks.

The TM motioned for quiet. Stopped.

I stepped up beside him on a raised platform. Together, we looked through a wall-slit and down into a room carved from stone.

In a single ray of sunlight, below, I saw two boys.

Caught motionless in a moment of play, the two looked intently at something. The slant of sunlight touched one boy's face. His cheek was devastatingly white—a blood condition—as though that beautiful forehead had never seen the sun. The face of the second boy was averted, was looking at something between them on the floor. The boy's head raised slightly. For one second the sun blazed like fire on his red hair.

Strangely, I was moved by the sight: young boys, alone, at play in a slant of sunlight.

I stepped down from the platform. At that moment, for me, this case was closed; aside, I whispered to my Town-Major, "Now, if they are clean, TM. Or, if they are your kin. Or if—"

Coldly, the Town-Major stared at me. Also whispering, he wished me to know they were indeed of his wife's family—but very distantly related. Very.

With new resolve the Town-Major went back to the observation platform. I joined him for I wished to look down again, to see two boys at play in sunlight.

Now they stood apart.

On the floor between them, I saw their very accurate model: a replica of the mine cart. Unmistakably it was so: axles, sides, a twig for the hand-brake rod, dried-clay wheels.

As I watched through the slit, the boy with red hair drew back his arm. On sun-baked wheels the little cart bumped once, then went wobbling, but very straight, as though on rails, went straight across the floor; and it carried truly its small load of small pebbles into the white-faced boy's waiting hand.

The boys laughed. In their re-echoing voices I heard the joy of invention with this new thing which they had made.

V

Down-river, past nightfall, the breeze was warm and our skiff slid hot between mudbanks; for one moment, all in a row, the tips of the oars caught the first moonlight.

What happened in Ochretown really was by the Manual (as revised): I did my job conscientiously; the

Town-Major did his. At the same time, however, the way he "managed" me illustrates both their national obsession and the reason no two days in the OMT are ever the same.

When we looked down into the Special-hold room, when I saw their small cart run on wheels of clay, for one long, attenuated moment my Town-Major said nothing at all. Then without hesitation, as though he saw something clearly, he turned and went back along the corridors.

Soon my TM came back, this time with two clay bowls of porridge, which was the late-afternoon meal. Through a smaller slit near the floor the Town-Major pushed the bowls into their room.

Unseen, silent, we watched from above: the boys ate their porridge. Greedily, they licked the bowls. Then they caused the bowls to run slowly on the rims: two wheels going in ever-smaller circles on the floor.

Patiently, we watched. In a little while the two boys became tired of this play; they laid down side by side as though to sleep. Because the cereal was drugged in the usual way, the boys soon were very much asleep in each other's arms—but were still breathing lightly.

Together we went into their cell. With my river boot I ground the clay-model cart and the wheels and the hand-brake into powder—a gesture. True, with the clay beneath my foot, I felt I had done something which was in some way disproportionate; at the same time it was a symbolic thing, a gesture for the benefit of my Town-Major.

Possibly my Town-Major also felt he should prove himself symbolically; or perhaps at that moment he wished to try my loyalty to him; or—more probably—it really is their obsession. In any event, he said almost patiently,

–Now you show Little Friend the sunlight? You *yako?*

Because we were alone, because very much I need the loyalty of all Town-Majors; because my trust in him was great; yes, and to confirm his own correct action in this case, I took from my concealed holster one of the two extant firearms in this entire Territory. One of my authorized pistols is at my Headquarters, well secured; the other firearm now rested lightly in my hand.

The Town-Major reached out his hand. He touched the gun.

I watched his face contort. His eyes became wide, startled, and then he smiled by drawing back his lips until—convulsively—he laughed.

Without having to be shown, without hesitation, as though all of his life it had been waiting for this, had remembered its role from some primordial, industrial past, the Town-Major's finger curled, found the trigger, and—by instinct—pulled.

Nothing happened.

Nothing happened until he was first above the boy with the pale face, and then legs astraddle above the boy with the red hair. Neither boy knew it or felt anything when I showed my TM an ultimate thing: a safety catch, how to press it, how to make the blue, loaded revolver— how to make it. Go.

In what manner the Town-Major disposed of two bodies and which details he told their mothers, I do not know.

In about three weeks, without having to ask, I received a half-levy of men from Ochretown; although their language is not known either to me or to my Coxswain, he feels—given time—they will become very good oarsmen.

Allegedly these men were taken from beyond my present Territory, from a valley where all through the night giant kilns throw flames of lavender and yellow against the low-hanging clouds. There being no rumors of metal, however, I shall neither seek that valley nor climb their escarpments of white, pure clay which are said to rear skyward somewhere to the West.

I was half-asleep but sitting upright when my Coxswain raised the first winking torch on our landing. Soon I saw the higher, bankside lights of my own Headquarter windows reflecting all in a row on the waters of a river which seems never to end.

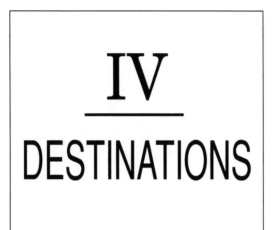

IV

DESTINATIONS

I Like It Better Now

I am no beauty, but I know auto parts. That's why I broke up so-called housekeeping in Oregon and came south to Los Angeles.

I'll say this for California: it's like anywhere else, so you take what you can get.

What I got was Ken's A/Z: an orange-front outlet of stucco that was once a Mom and Pop grocery and before that a realty office with some room for parking in the rear. Ken's auto parts is mostly a Ford and GM place with not a grille or a piece of chrome on the shelf.

Our A to Z customers wanted only to get to a job if they had one, and then to make it back to the Buckville off-ramp near Palmetto. And if some Chicanos regularly collected five dollars from Asa at the back ramp for a generator that still smelled like sparks, it was no business of mine.

Ken's was that kind of place: a necessary kind of retarded 1930s place right in the middle of "Everchanging Los Angeles" as they say. Especially those late, summer afternoons the smog got so bad our neon sign came on, and blinked, and turned my face off and on in two shades of purple.

The first month at A to Z I learned plenty.

Ken, that sweetheart, priced all our parts 20 percent above let's say "suggested retail" and in that way he sold on credit, and lots of it. Ken sold to anyone who claimed a fixed address or who could remember almost any telephone number, more often than not a bar. At first I was surprised to see so many women customers with tiny little children: those women bought radiator hose and clamps and tune-up kits, signed-off for credit, and put the parts in a stroller with the baby. A lot of these women, especially black women, were doing their own repair work; you could tell by the way they bought. I guess if the family hack is running in the break-down lane, then someone can't get to work. I've seen them go out the door, baby teething on a hose clamp, and it would break your heart.

I still think Ken's real trouble was the freckle-elbow guys from Oklahoma or Texas or Georgia—individuals something like himself. When those rougher elements came in, sometimes half-dusted up, Asa faded back into our stockrooms, him being black.

I kept the front counter between me and them, and if some knuckle buster ordered a nonexistent part—like a head-clutch holder—I'd say, "Waste my time, Smokey Bear, and I'll tighten your shimmy bolt."

Asa being a Negro—I mean, a black person—he knew best all our Negro trade. Asa was a great deal more than your normal parts jockey; he did a lot of Ken's buying at the back door. In addition, Asa knew where his accounts, mostly Negroes, actually lived.

As will be seen, I got to respect and to like Asa Bowers a lot. Even so, at the desk I usually worked anything that was white and tattooed.

Quite a while later, Asa told me he knew my way of talking to the knuckle busters was only to protect myself—and my job. Also, being once married himself, Asa understood how it could be for any woman in a new town, especially around Boyle Heights. I'm saying that Asa understood what he saw.

Anyway, Asa worked the stockrooms and was real "dumb" about hot stuff at the back door. I held down my end at the parts counter and some bookkeeping—except for Asa's special-contact accounts, or "his people" as that sweetheart Ken always put it.

Working together like that, you get to know a person and I got to know Asa. Even if I was a little bit older and a little bit lonely at first, I never did remotely give Asa no hints the way some Oregon women do—mentioning no names in public.

But nothing mattered: A/Z burned, and I'll never see Asa Bowers again. Whether he was good or bad or just mixed, I don't care to know, but probably I lost a friend.

As for Ken: took Jane, his wife, and left for somewhere back East, Ohio. The orange front and all that neon is gone—and I have a better job. But when you see a junker blowing a hose on the freeway in all that airport traffic, say this: he's running A/Z parts on Ken's E/Z credit—and not paid for yet.

To this day I don't remember when Asa first mentioned his Dodge, his personal automobile. Probably we talked about it when eating our take-out Chinese on the back ramp.

After I invited him two or three times, Asa did come up to my place after work; even if a woman is older and is no beauty it is only natural to want some kind of company. Probably we talked auto parts, including his '68 Dodge four-door which I never did see, as it turned out.

As I am no talker, I did not at first tell Asa everything.

On the other hand, if he put it all together, Asa would know our graduating class at Eastfir Junction (Oregon) was forty-six in all. But he would not know as of graduation that of twenty girls, twelve were pregnant and two maybe.

I had been dating Ollie mostly because he was the star, but I saw where too much parking in a pickup truck did lead. Because Ollie was a star, he went to logging for Union Ply; I wanted to go on to secretarial school. Then all at once there were fourteen marriages in Eastfir Junction, and because I am not and was not overly pretty, and because Ollie had his job and asked me again, there seemed no reason why not make it fifteen in a row for Eastfir.

We went up to Portland for our honeymoon, and then set up housekeeping in a mobile home park.

Nothing happened for three years. We went to more Elks' dances, round and square, than I care to remember. Then being hung over as usual on a Monday morning while setting chokers, Ollie was hurt. He had to quit logging and I was sorry; his right leg would always be stiff at the knee joint. I guess everyone who works in the woods eventually gets hurt, but Ollie did draw Compensation.

People felt sorry for Ollie because he played good basketball for Eastfir, so he got work in the shop at the White Truck and Plymouth Agency. Everyone meant well, but Ollie Mateson was handy only with a ball. He became a halfway-mechanic, with one finger always in a splint.

No children.

After a while I was just as glad because I did not want to sit in the Eagles' club rooms and listen to old basketball scores or how Cy Frederics limited out the first forty minutes of trout season in '60. Unless I had to bring Ollie home, I never entered any tavern without an escort. Would I could say the same for a few of the girls in my graduation class—mentioning no names.

Finally what happened was I learned auto parts.

Our trailer park was near the Agency. To help Ollie draw his full time, I began to help out at the parts counter. In a year I was working full time on my own card. If you are accurate, and can read the specs, and are fast, I suppose anyone can learn auto parts. But when is the last time you saw a woman who really knew her stuff on log trucks?

Fact was Ollie got pretty far down, even for Eastfir Junction. Sometimes out a week, drinking his Compensation; other times, after being on my feet all day, I'd go home and eat by myself while someone that was legally my husband slept it off in the bedroom.

In late summer, I filed divorce papers and caught the first bus south for California. Ollie never knew I was gone until payday, and not one girl in my high-school class ever dropped me a line.

"Oh, you had to leave," was what Asa said when we were sitting around in my living room after I had cooked us a real good meal.

Asa repaid hospitality in two ways. He fixed anything that went wrong, plumbing or electrical; he was the kind of mechanic that looks at something and knows what's wrong. As our shop posters said, Asa was "safety-minded." When he fixed a toaster it didn't afterward blow up in a shower of sparks. His second way was conversation. Asa told me about all those children in Watts where the schools hadn't served a hot lunch in years; he told me about the families over on Palmetto and the men who drive eighty miles on the freeway to their work. Before, I never knew you couldn't catch any bus from there and get to a job before 10:00 A.M., which even in Los Angeles is too late. Before I had not understood how important an automobile was: parts from Ken's A/Z were more necessary than groceries.

As it turned out, Asa's own '68 Dodge sedan was parked in a vacant lot. It didn't run well, he said, but it was too good for junk.

So there we were, four flights up, talking until half past ten at night with the lights of the city spread out toward the Hollywood hills and the freeway traffic rolling overhead, the hum of tires and wheels rising and falling like the noise of some big, metal insect trying to get away.

"Sure, Ruthie," Asa told me one night about eleven o'clock as he was going very quietly towards the door. "You were a good woman. Back in Oregon nobody saw that."

After Asa left, I wanted to cry, but no one was around to hear me.

II

For what happened that summer, which was long after the Watts riots and fires, I blame no one but Ken, also his wife.

I'll say this for Asa: he seldom spoke about himself, but by putting things together, I understood he grew up in Lexington, Kentucky. Asa never saw his father but Kilroy was there all right because Asa's mother got five more kids from someplace. I don't say children is wrong but I do say a house like that had its ill effects especially on Asa being old enough to understand what he saw.

Asa lacked my advantages since he dropped out of high school after three years and three months; on the other hand, he served his time in the Army in a second-echelon motor pool. For a year or two nothing hap-

pened in Lexington, so Asa went to Chicago to work for
an office building. At first he ran the elevator but when
pumps in the basement began to go out Asa helped on
maintenance. It cost plenty to keep that old building in
shape, just in plumbing and electrical.

Asa ended up doing all maintenance, but another colored veteran got all the credit. When some hydraulics
broke, the elevator fell two floors to the bumper and Asa
got fired.

What Asa said about the lady in the case is this: she
was from Chicago, a sub in the post office—which was
good money when she got it. I understand she was
somewhat lighter in color than Asa, and since he never
mentioned even a civil marriage ceremony or a honeymoon, I ignored that subject, it being well in the past.

Asa took what he could get at the time in the way of
work: a washrack or part time for the City hauling snow
off the streets. Since nothing was steady, Asa did not
expect to draw his full time. This next, however, I con-
sider unreasonable.

What his wife—we will call her—wanted was children. Children was all she talked: how many her friends
had, how many were pregnant, how she was getting
older, and etc. What Asa wanted was a job, and children
would naturally follow; then his wife said, "Which
comes first, the chicken or the pot?"

Asa had to tell her it was wrong, in his experience, to
bring kids into the world with no visible means of sup-
port. Almost every night they left it like that.

After a while, Asa saw he, himself, was one of the
"chronic unemployed" he read about in the papers.
Knowing Asa, I would say he tried, but on Monday it
always seemed to rain, on Tuesday the work week had
already started, and on Wednesday night his wife went
to the movies with her lady friends. To help out, Asa

taught himself to cook, but being a sub, she came back from the post office feeling put on by the regulars. When she got up from the table, she always said, "Tell me this. Which came first?"

Then this superintendent of mails—older somewhat—asked the wife into his postal section on a regular-employee basis; Asa got the picture because then his wife did not come home except on Sunday afternoons.

Asa got so far down on himself he didn't even go around to see the man about it.

Asa had his '68 Dodge, so after the elevator dropped, Asa loaned the Dodge to his wife's younger brother.

One day Asa borrowed back his own automobile from the brother, and by midnight was through Des Moines, headed for California.

Asa said it himself: in Chicago the lady in the case is now a lot better off than with a chronic unemployed sitting all day looking out the window.

"But you take all of *that*," Asa said one night, meaning sex, because we were talking about both the lady in the case and about Ollie. "Isn't that just one little part of life?"

"Of that, I'm sure," I said, for such was my experience.

Now I'm *supposed* to be different. Even women who ought to know better often believe that.

Not knowing, I said nothing at all.

"But we aren't," Asa said, and his voice trailed back across the years to Chicago. "Not me," and he looked down into the pattern of my new rug. "I never was very good. At that."

Asa was feeling things that went back to Lexington, and five kids in a shack at the edge of town. I thought he was both brave and real honest to admit things like that about himself; for any man, something like that is not easy to face. I saw one thing very clear: Asa had lost confidence in himself and what Asa needed was to get it back.

Of a sudden I saw it: if we got his automobile in shape, then Asa would have two things going. He'd have wheels, and on Sundays could ride the range clear out to Riverside, or similar. Second, a '68 was all right, and in two years would be a Classic.

People in L.A., especially Oakies and Texans and some Chicanos, have got Classic on the brain. I say it is all iron from Detroit, but if it's "old" and shines, they buy it for "an investment," they say.

Well, the first thing you know we talked headers and a gutted muffler and maybe going across into Mexico for a tuck-and-roll job on the upholstery. The more Asa said had to be done, the more we laughed and laughed until we couldn't laugh anymore.

"We need," I said, "to pry the license plates apart. Then put a new car in between."

That's an old one, but we laughed again. That night when Asa got ready to leave, I thought the freeway traffic overhead almost stopped, but of course it never does. When Asa hesitated overly long at the door, he was no longer even smiling.

"Let's don't mention this. To Ken?"

"Oh?" because I am aboveboard with any firm that hires me, E/Z Credit or no. "Wouldn't he discount us employees? Wouldn't it just be another open account? For Ken?"

Asa did not answer me on that, and he did not look me in the eye.

"I'd rather not," he said finally, and I felt he lacked confidence in himself. "For personal reasons . . ."

At the time, I thought this: Asa being only our stock-person, as they say, he was naturally cautious; he did not want Ken to know the two of us were friendly.

As will be seen, that sweetheart Ken was not always reasonable about automobile parts.

I respected Asa's judgment and did not wish to hurt his feelings, so I said, "Okay. We run this one in Lo. I'll carry all our parts on my own personal account. You pay me something, every week or so. That way it's regular."

Asa seemed a little relieved.

"Yes. Just right. Your account, like an investment."

And that's exactly the way we left it.

III

Comes October: I showed for work and both Ken and his wife Jane were already waiting at A/Z.

I had to knock twice, just to get in.

That was a Friday.

"If The Ace shows," Ken called from one of the back rooms where he was wrestling with a ladder, "call me."

"Ruthie," Jane said, "we are pulling Inventory. Right now."

I put the CLOSED, SORRY WE MISSED YOU sign in the window, and laced into my smock; Ken began his count, from the top shelves down.

Before long, Ken began to count and to cuss: away down, he kept saying, why I'm away down on all Jimmy parts, meaning GM. And Dodge parts. I can see that already.

The more stuff Ken counted the madder he got. Finally he was yelling down at his wife, "Jane, can't you even write down my numbers?"

So much for the whole morning, and no Asa as yet.

At 2 P.M., with no break, I took off the smock.

If Ken wouldn't say it, I could:

"Slip into Neutral, Ken. I'll go get your sandwich. You want relish or mustard?"

While waiting at the drive-in, I decided—like it or not—Ken had to know. The fact was that I had billed out plenty of parts for Asa's '68 Dodge. I would show all my invoices when the time came, clear and aboveboard: no hard feelings.

Back at A/Z, what I heard was Ken. He was yelling at Asa.

From the front door I see Asa in the stockroom, his body slanted sideways in the light.

"Why, at my bowling alley," Ken said, "everyone down there knows you are peddling on the side."

I went right on to the back room to settle that one.

"Mr. Ken," and when Asa saw me standing in the stockroom door he nodded Hello, but his lips moved only a little when he went on speaking.

"Let's not, Mr. Ken, confuse my personal car with our bad credit accounts."

"Ace, you been peddling my parts all over Palmetto."

"No, sir. Every one is bolted on my Dodge. I'll show you every one."

Ken spit on the floor and rubbed it in with his shoe sole.

"You are collecting, Ace, but not for me. Your people aren't paid up to me."

I saw the reason Asa knew so much about our Palmetto Avenue accounts: if Asa steered them into A/Z, he also had to collect each week. I had not quite realized that.

"I get what's there," Asa said. "You ought to collect more from your own big-ticket customers."

Asa had a point: Ken was all sell and real weak on collections.

"You damned right," Ken said, and he began to throw papers and invoices and four-colored brochures from Gulf & Western on the floor.

"But there's money on Palmetto. I know it. If you can't collect it, I can. The hard way."

"I work for *you*." Asa said quietly. "I advise against that. You don't know . . . what might happen."

Ken didn't even listen to what Asa was saying.

"Gents," I said, and walked between them, to break it up. "One thing I'll show you both," and I opened the drawer of the file cabinet.

My personal account—all my invoices for all those Dodge and a great many more other parts—were gone.

Without actually shaking his head, Asa very plainly told me, "No. Don't say anything."

Asa, someway, had lifted my file, to protect my job. Even then I would have told it all, but Ken turned on me.

"You going to count, or are you going to roost? I'll repo that Dodge. Just any time."

With that, Asa seemed to shrink down inside himself. His little sideways slouch said a very great deal. Asa was all through, so Ken moved in on him.

"Ace, what's that thing? Right over there?"

"That's the door," Asa said. "And I'm going out."

Asa did not look back. Beyond the loading ramp he went down steps as though he were going off into deep water. His head disappeared. The door closed by itself.

"What The Ace was," Ken's wife said, after she finished her sandwich, "was a parts-booster, a good-time boy. And he had way too many friends."

For the first time I doubted Asa.

For a fact did he own that '68 Dodge sedan? Did he allow me to put everything he used on my account so that—just technically—he wasn't stealing from stock?

Even though I did not want to think about it, I knew I had brought it all on myself.

"Up in Oregon," Ken said, and he had to speak again to bring me out of it. "Up in the woods. Ever drive a pickup truck?"

That's what I did the rest of the afternoon. I drove Ken's pickup while Jane called out the address and how much all of Asa's accounts owed Ken's A/Z.

I drove us along Palmetto, and on into Watts. I stopped at house trailers and stucco houses and apartments; I stopped at places where nobody lived, and I drove through alleys, and over the curbs, and into vacant lots. Wherever we stopped, Ken jumped down from the truck. He knocked on doors, and went into garages, or up the stairs past garbage cans. He found their Fords, Chevs, and old Pontiacs; we even spotted a blue Caddie parked beneath trees, the seat cushions kicked out on the street. So Ken took them, too.

At every car Ken repossessed something. He pulled a battery, or an air cleaner, or someone's carburetor; he took a spare tire from a trunk. He even pulled a set of ignition wires off the loom. He kicked and slammed and used a wrecking bar; sometimes if the account was long overdue, Ken took an inside mirror or even a fan belt. At every old car the kids stood in a half-circle to watch and their mothers looked down from apartment windows; Jane helped Ken, and we drove away quickly and no one complained and not one person called the police.

Finally we drove back to A/Z.

I parked us at the back ramp and Ken threw all the repo stuff by the door in a disorganized, greasy pile. After Ken unloaded the last battery, Jane looked at the junk pile.

"If they couldn't hump it," she said, "then why buy it in the first place?"

When I saw all those parts—repossessed, stripped—I thought of all the cars that could not get men to work come Monday morning. Some of those cars kept a man working, made him the true head of a family.

Then Jane mentioned Asa's name for the last time.

"The Ace could sell all right," she said. "But he couldn't collect shit with a shingle."

Ken said, "Good field, no hit."

"Keep counting," I told both of them, and untied my last smock for A/Z. "I'm headed for home. To get off my feet."

Ken locked the door behind me when I left.

IV

Towards midnight I was looking out my window. In downtown Los Angeles it was one of your warm October nights when the smog is withdrawn but you know at dawn the exhaust fumes and the day's heat will make the inversion layer slam down again like a heavy, grey, stove lid.

Someone knocked—not very loud.

It was Asa. He'd come back. He was standing in the door, and then he was standing in my living room.

Asa looked neat, and he was neat. For the first time I saw him dressed: a tan shirt and the right kind of narrow tie, a good-looking suit, and a brown snap-brim straw hat . . . traveling clothes . . .

Without asking my permission, Asa turned off all my lights.

Suddenly my new drapes and my TV and my couch

and even Asa and me turned to silver-grey in the light reflected up from the boulevard.

"I have been out," Asa told me. "Around Palmetto. I explained to most of them. To my accounts."

"Ken's not going to get beat," I said. "And she's worse."

"Oh, he blames the colored," Asa said. "But his First National Bank is pressing. And all of his suppliers."

"Asa," I said, and that is when I reached out in the semi-darkness and touched his hand. I felt so sad. Yet it was also a funny feeling to touch a hand like that for the first time—not cold, but not warm either. We stood like that for only a moment; I knew I ought to say something, but I said the wrong thing.

"Did you use *all* those parts on the Dodge? The ones I gave you?"

Too late, I understood how that sounded to Asa. He drew back, and so did I. I heard Asa take a deep breath but whatever he might of said never came out in words.

Far away, then closer, we heard sirens. Closer they came, the lights and the sirens bleeding red noise along the street.

Two blocks away, unmistakably at Ken's A/Z, we saw flames. First it was a glow between two large buildings. Then the whole sky seemed to blow up. Windows and the white walls of the buildings glowed orange and then red, as though the fire were climbing up, and across rooftops, and to the hills of Hollywood beyond. Below us the street filled with people running: Chicanos, and whites, and blacks, and children, and women with children in their arms all going along the sidewalks towards the big fire at Ken's A/Z.

"I told him," Asa said. "I advised Ken: don't collect like that."

"Over on Palmetto. Did they tell you? Say they were going to burn us down?"

"Someone set it," and Asa smiled a little because in a way everyone likes to see a fire, in the woods in Oregon or down here in Buckville not far from Watts.

I did not know what to say. I thought of all our customers: Filipinos, some Chinese, guys from Wake or Pango Pango; and some from Georgia, and Texas, and Oklahoma. Rednecks, drunks, dopers, SSI, anyone who had the freeway system on their backs, who had to get somewhere, anywhere.

"Not any of us," Asa said, and he sensed what I was thinking. "None of us would do a thing like that. Not for a used fan belt."

I believed what Asa said because I wanted to believe.

"That's oil burning," he said. "Knuckle busters from Oklahoma always use oil. They already got their big ticket items. Insurance company pays for them . . ."

I believed that as well. Ken would collect, right out of the ashes.

"Or old Honk-Ken, himself," Asa said bitterly. "That's why he pulled inventory. This morning."

I thought that, too, was possible.

"Maybe no one will ever know who set it," Asa went on. "But I know this. They will look for the nigger. The nigger that just got fired. For stealing."

Again I did not say anything because I thought Asa was right.

"And wouldn't the nigger be me? For sure?" and before I could say anything, or even say I was sorry, Asa slammed my own door in my face.

Well, Asa never knew it but I just stood there and listened to his footsteps go farther and farther down my stairs, and then pause at the bottom landing.

I think he paused to look up and down the street.

Then the downstairs door slammed, but I never did see him walk away.

I went back to my window and stood there and watched for a long time.

Finally the last fire engine went away, about two-thirty in the morning.

As I said, Ken went back East, to Ohio. Whether or not he collected insurance no one ever said. Just privately, I'd say he scored; that's how Ken got out of town.

In no time at all, with a good resume, I got me a better job with this volume dealer on Wilshire. I like it here because I am much closer in to Hollywood.

Sometimes, beyond our show-window on the sidewalk, I see Michael, or Richard Burton, and other notables. Naturally they don't do any of their own work, so they never come in for our fast, accurate service and ALL major credit cards honored.

Also I like it better because I work only my forty hours per week and good benefits. I haven't seen a freckled elbow yet, and we wouldn't let a used fan belt in the house. We write up plenty of chrome and grilles, and if you say the word, you got yourself a one-piece, tinted, wrap-around windshield for GM products exclusive.

I'm saying we also wholesale to the fender and body shops, the real pros.

As for so-called race relations, it's like I tell my Parts Foreman, a kid they trained at the factory who doesn't know a head-clutch holder from a rollicking rod but who is real safety minded:

"Look, Smokey Bear, I got plenty of mileage left on the chassis. I'm just getting a little hard to start in the morning."

A Circle of Friends

I'm saying in my case the Social Security people went for this one:

A shrink's *opinion* about me being a vet and my values and my lifestyle here on the coast in California and you should get out here sometime.

Secondly, mailed in from Niles, Michigan, my Xeroxed "up-date" of my (same name) father's more-or-less arranged diagnosis of epilepsy, which he claimed at the time.

For epilepsy you have to show just one event; it's real dangerous to drive if you got it.

Anyway, I'm back at Tampico #2, and Merriweather is still hung up somewhere's beyond Grass Valley, also California.

Actually, before I drove us over the Pass to the remote-vista A-frame, I knew Merriweather pretty well. She was doing back-up for Lou-Robin at Tampico #2, all women bartenders, Happy Hour from ten A.M. onward. Lots of us vets hang out there.

From my place at the end of the bar I bought; then

Merriweather bought back. Her being temporary help, no harm done—ask anybody.

Twice we made the horses at Golden Gate. Once I broke even.

Probably I passed out this side of San Jose, but Merriweather brought the Pontiac on in. The next day at 10:00 A.M., we opened the Tampico Deuce per usual and were off-and-running, if you see what I mean.

Astrology's a laugh, but here's actually the way finally we decided our trip to that remote-vista A-frame: my SSI check's due the 3d; also the 3d, Lou-Robin could catch a double-header at Candlestick Park. Twice three is six and that equalled Merriweather's six-day roll through Friday. This friend's friend's A-frame was empty—also a dog to be fed. So I said if no chains required, we take the Pontiac. Which we did.

For a guy thirty-five years old such as myself and not thinning too much on top if I comb it forward, the Pontiac is all right: over one hundred thousand miles, never had the heads off, and good for another fifteen; I can patch that muffler myself because I have all my own tools.

Also, my place is at #27 Acey, one block, very convenient, from Tampico #2. From outside it looks informal, but welfare pays 80 percent of my rent; inside, if you sit hard on the couch, you still won't see any black velocipedes—I call them that—run up the wall. Above my TV are the books. The one "book" is actually my jock-box, where I keep my Marksman's Medal and fifty or seventy-five dollars in cash at all times.

When I deal it is only grass, and only to friends, and only for personal use.

Naturally, I'm not all roses. Those two drunk-driving violations and also leaving-the-scene were my own damned fault. And once they drafted me, I pulled Basic and I hit Marksman because in Niles my father (now passed away) familiarized all the kids with guns, including my oldest sister who now drives her own eighteen-wheel rig.

I could have scored Sharpshooter except I wasn't used to Texas crosswinds. Anyway, I thought they didn't train me anyways near well enough to get on any airplane headed for Nam: I ducked, and when it was almost over, I turned myself in at the downtown Waco Recruiting Station. I ended up with pretty good papers and ever since I've registered Democrat—just in case.

I'm saying this Merriweather—Hauk, her name was and still is—knew my philosophy pretty well. Also I'm saying I knew Merriweather better than you would think I would. From my spot at the end of the bar just watching her relate to my circle of friends tells you a lot about a woman's personal philosophy.

I read her like this: for Merriweather this remote-vista A-frame trip was both a way to get out of town, like self-interest; also a relationship test-out, us being alone. Sex had nothing to do with it, and although Merriweather made that sort of clear at the time, even now I don't know if she really meant it—regards sex, I mean.

I do know, however, very much she wanted to feed that dog. So I'd say on balance Merriweather kept after me, and finally I said, the Pontiac is ready when you are.

And that's why we decided to go up and across the Pass to this remote-vista A-frame of a friend's friend.

II

Saturday night Merriweather slept at #27 Acey to get an early departure. Sunday morning Merriweather was up at eight and accidentally found a Vodka bottle cooling behind my ice-cube trays. Probably her quart of grapefruit juice came from Tampico #2 in her big Mexican purse because Lou-Robin never did show up, and Merriweather took over.

After a couple of GJ & V eye-openers, I said, Long's won't be open until 10:00 A.M. and for Bourbon back-up, oughten we fill out the case of a Buckmeister Springs at those prices? Also, get six quarts of oil because the Bonnie will blow smoke on the Pass.

One thing led to another. We departed past noon, and I thought Merriweather might have managed a little better. After all, she went two years to a community college.

Finally on the road: all Vodka and a full case of Buckmeister Springs and also everything else with the seal broken; Lou-Robin's sleepbag; some boxes of carry-out Chinese food; some half-and-half Hi-Protein for the dog. All of that *inside* the trunk.

I am flying left-seat, gliding along on Grapefruit Juice and Vodka, straight up.

She is about my age, maybe four years younger. The scar down and across her right cheek is from an automobile wreck that killed the other two women; at the time Merriweather wasn't driving. Before that she had a boyfriend who volunteered and got snuffed in Nam.

Some Wednesdays Merriweather volunteered to watch at this day-care center, Lou-Robin having one kid there by a previous arrangement. Anyway, Merriweather was, I could tell, somewhat excited to be gliding along in the right seat. For our first real trip she was wearing a gold ring in her left ear and also one in her right nostril, which was pierced but not for regular use. She looked okay, and I told her so.

Privately, however, I read Merriweather like this:

First, I had said, No chains on the Pass; then I said, We take the Pontiac; then I said, All Vodka and Buckmeister Springs and anything else and all bottles with the seal broken packed and locked *inside* the Pontiac trunk; then I said, Kick Off at eight A.M., sharp.

All those things made Merriweather understand this thing was organized; all she needed now was the friend's map. My philosophy is this: somebody has to be in charge, and she appreciated that.

Beyond San Jose, just past the closed-down GM Assembly Plant, I parked us on the berm. I unlocked the trunk as though inspecting the Chinese take-out and Merriweather topped us off with GJ & V because it was That Time.

"Up in the mountains will be nice," Merriweather said when I got the Pontiac back to economic-cruise past Walnut Creek.

"They better be," I said. "After all, we are feeding the damned dog—if he is still there."

Then in my opinion Merriweather said something very down:

"Ron—Uh. Ron, we didn't leave until afternoon. Will we get over the Pass? Before dark?"

I heard what she said and I heard her flinch and I knew why: every mile towards the Pass was a mile farther from our circle of friends; so Merriweather was a little scared and that's probably why she dressed up and wore both gold rings. For the same reason she wanted to buy a Los Angeles *Times* Sunday Edition, "for reading matter." But I said, We are going *north*. And we might need our cash for gas.

Past Sacramento, she was slumped down in the right seat. From time to time she got the friend's map out of her Mexican handbag, turned the map this way and that.

Finally I said, Look: our ETA is 4:30—more or less.

If that fucking map of yours is right, I'll be there before dark. Okay?

Well, maybe I did call a rest-stop at Quoit Junction. Also one for Merriweather at a smaller place. Also we stopped for some of the Chinese take-out, which was still warm from the trunk heat. Also I found this Arco station—twice.

But like I said: if her map was right, I would have found that A-frame a lot sooner than any 10:00 P.M.

Finally, at the end of "Road marked McCormik," I parked.

By the trunk-light I saw Merriweather had thrown in two sheets and two pillows and some underwear change for me, which sort of told me how she might be thinking.

The path to the A-frame was up-hill and I carried sufficient supplies, mostly Vodka, and left the back-up supplies, the Buckmeister Springs, *locked* in the trunk.

No dog on guard.

No lights, no electricity turned on in the A-frame.

No dog inside the A-frame, but we had his Hi-Protein.

Outside on the deck Merriweather called and called. Her voice carried downwind into the valley. No dog.

"Let the sonofabitch live off the land," I said, and in the dark tried to clear a place on the floor to sleep.

Finally Merriweather came inside. Accidentally she found the A-frame breakers: wham, lights.

Right then I saw why this A-frame smelled dog.

Merriweather took the gold ring out of her nose and out of her earlobe. "Tomorrow we will . . . maybe straighten it out."

So we had a couple of Vodka Nightcaps and spread Lou-Robin's sleepbag on the floor. I thought she brought them up to the A-frame, but I guess Merriweather left our bedsheets in the Pontiac.

III

Next morning, a Monday. Merriweather got up and I got up.

We stepped out on a frost-covered deck: treetops down a narrow valley of stone and beyond, in the haze, another valley, and sometimes a flash of light on the windshield of a log truck going down.

Behind and below the A-frame, where her map stopped, the Pontiac was half-inside some acacia bushes, where I dropped the hook. Thirty feet beyond the acacias, the road stopped. The tracks just dropped off a cliff.

Two hundred feet below the cliff I saw pigbacks of granite grunting in the sun. No dog.

Previous parties unknown, however, probably by accident, had locked the dog *inside* the cabin. So the dog had to eat all the chair upholstery and a floor mattress, and in the heat clawed down the sunshades looking for water. Later parties unknown probably let him out.

After Merriweather got the dog-clawed mattress and two chairs, and all the empty beer cans and dog shit out on the deck, I told her, Just push it over the side and if it rains hard enough, even the dog shit is biodegradable.

Our take-out Chinese was finished, but in the loft I found fifteen cans of Campbell's soup, "Tomato 'N Rice." For lunch we passed one can back and forth with Vodka Chasers and used the same spoon, which was the only utensil found.

We woke up later, just about the time our circle of friends would be kicking off Tampico Deuce. So it was Here's to Your Old Remote Vista and I did the honors (straight up). Sometime later the sun held for one minute on the treetops then spilled shadows into the valley until the A-frame was the last point of light at the cliff's edge. Then it was cold and dark. We did another can of Tomato 'N Rice and sometime later got ourselves zipped into the sleepbag, clothes and all.

Same Tuesday, same Wednesday, same Thursday, same Friday, except at about our Happy Hour the sky beyond the deck became dark. A gust of hail hit the deck like a thousand thrown, bounding dice, then disappeared.

All at once, at the same time, both of us saw something. Merriweather saw it, and then I saw it.

Both of us laughed and laughed, me included.

It was all there and always had been: wood, stacked along the wall; a sheetmetal fireplace with screen; a square bottle of kerosene; a square box of fireplace matches. Before we didn't put those things together, and we slept cold all night.

In a minute we built a fire. We sat there, and we looked at the flames, and we glided along on Buckmeister Springs and Branch, our fall-back supplies. Outside the rain broke across the A-frame roof; inside, real safe, we just glided along talking.

"Sure, I'm SSI. But one thing . . .

Merriweather was looking deep into the fire.

"No needle ever humped my veins."

"I awisht," Merriweather said, "I could say that, I do."

"Except medically prescribed. Or at parties. Or just skin-pops."

"I don't think drugs . . . anymore."

"And no debts—also my philosophy."

"I wisht I could say that. About home."

Her remark told me why Merriweather never mentioned the two of us driving back to her town in Illinois, where her stepfather owns his own welding shop, and maybe needed a Helper. Also I know this: with good letters, at first, a woman can get home-money; later, you can't depend on it—which is not like SSI.

"I owe no man," I said, "and here's your branch vista."

Actually my bankruptcy in '79 taught me a lot about credit and individual relationships, and I don't count GI loans, as in Basic Training when some of my company got on the airplane. If they came back, and if they used their heads, why they took any and all loans to me as tax write-offs.

"If . . ." and I heard all this regret penned up inside her, "could . . . manage."

I didn't say anything. When it comes to regret, I won't discuss it; it gets just too damned personal.

Our logs burned, and nobody said anything. We took turns getting supplies which was Bucky S. & B., and then about eleven o'clock the wind really hit the roof and the fireplace puffed smoke and the stovepipe swayed as we watched.

Now the A-frame smelled better. We had four more cans of Tomato 'N Rice on the shelf. We were close-wrapped in Lou-Robin's bag. So I changed the subject: to something more or less on both our minds.

Right away Merriweather got my meaning.

"Ron . . . Ronald . . ." and then Merriweather said, "You wouldn't like that. And it's caused me . . . so much . . . trouble."

I couldn't understand that: you have some pleasures in life besides Golden Gate Fields and the horses, I said.

"It's not you. It's me."

"Sure as Hell is."

"Last year I said never again—forever. If I feel that way, Lou-Robin says, I am better off that way—forever."

And that's the way Merriweather flinched, and after using my Pontiac all the way up here really just to feed some non-existent dog. Merriweather is Catholic or something because only a Nun or something would say, "Forever."

Real abrupt, Merriweather stood up. She started to tend to business. She put two logs on the fire; she started putting all empty bottles in rows. I wasn't sore, but after driving all the way up here, at the least we could taken off our clothes.

Actually, I'll never know exactly what happened later that night.

Probably Merriweather more or less joined me in a couple of Nightcaps, B. S. & B., or just straight. Had we been back at the old Tampie Deuce with our circle of friends—like Fronz, and The Starr; like Auto Apeman, and even Lou-Robin—why we would have closed it. Pretty much we closed it down anyway. No more Bucky-baby, and our fire was out.

Looking back on it, I'd say about 3:00 A.M., or so I told the deputy.

Probably Merriweather woke up because of the storm, and thought to set out some Tomato 'N Rice for Doggie. Anyway, she was walking and walking, but she forgot something: no Bucky Springs, no supplies. Now of course we *had* supplies, but they were down in the Pontiac.

I never said it because the deputy never asked me, but maybe I did hear Merriweather say to someone, "I'll get it. It's my turn."

So I rolled over to wait, but Merriweather didn't come back right away, so I probably slept, the rain having increased some. Being SSI, I have to watch it; besides, maybe she wanted to sleep alone in the Pontiac, that being her philosophy.

By morning, about Kick Off, I got up. I saw Merriweather never had come back because her Tomato 'N Rice was unopened on the counter.

One thing sure: all remaining supplies in the Pontiac, so Merriweather should get back up here soon and I knew she was thinking the same thing.

I also thought this: someone has to get this thing organized because Lou-Robin expected Merriweather back yesterday, or maybe by this evening. Also the Pontiac needed gas and oil and also check the tires for going over the Pass.

So I found my sandals and walked down to the Pontiac to get this thing organized. Pontiac locked: trunk locked, also the doors. Merriweather had my only set of automobile keys, but this time she got it right: trunk locked, also doors locked.

Maybe in the dark at 3:00 A.M. she walked past the acacia bushes and on down the two-track road. I followed the road. Around the first curve, I met a dog.

The dog was parked between two wheel tracks, mouth open, panting as though he wanted a drink. I took one friendly step, but the dog hit the underbrush, scared.

"Dog," I said, "you just missed your Hi-Protein."

I turned back to the A-frame and then I thought to look in front of the acacias.

And there she was.

Either Merriweather got in the Pontiac to sleep and then had to go to the bathroom in the dark—as I told the deputy later; or, she got her supplies and didn't forget to lock everything, and in the dark walked right over the cliff.

There she was: below was straight down, two hundred feet, and nothing but granite pigbacks and little pine trees. All the way down and that was the end . . .

Merriweather was on the face of the cliff, only down about twenty feet.

She was wedged between granite and a single scrub-pine. She was face up, twisted, wedged tight. Her arms were outspread as though still falling. Wedged between her shoulder and the granite cliff was—supplies, a Fifth of Bucky Springs. In her outstretched right hand, sparkling in the sun, my car keys.

I stood there, tried to get this thing organized.

Naturally, it was a miracle: six inches either way and Merriweather would have gone end-over-end into the pigbacks of granite.

To think of it made me shake and then—very odd for me—I couldn't stop shaking. Probably because of the cold.

Beneath my sandals, at the cliff's edge, was a half-path. Very steep. Real narrow. I'm SSI, so I have to watch it, and once down there to get my keys, maybe I couldn't pick my way back.

Finally, I had no choice and I hated to do it. With a fist-sized rock, on the driver's side, I broke my own car window. Once inside the Pontiac, I went through the back seat cushions and into the trunk. Sure enough: one supply left. I bit the seal off in the trunk with my teeth—it being cold.

Behind the spare tire was the fishing reel and line and some small trout hooks. Some friends forgot them in the trunk and I forgot to give them back.

Soon I hooked up the car keys from Merriweather Hauk's outstretched, half-opened hand—and probably saved her life.

From the first pay-telephone, I told the sheriff's office where this emergency was and I would meet them right here: at this Arco station.

After an hour, I was leading a sheriff's deputy named Ralph, one wrecker, and one ambulance unit, back towards the A-frame.

At the acacia bush we parked all in a row. As later stated in the report, I led our rescue party to the accident site.

This Hauk girl was still down there, wedged between the granite cliff and the only scrub-pine along the whole face: eyes closed, arms still outstretched.

Ralph the Deputy looked down over the cliff and said, "She shouldn't ought to move. Any."

This Deputy Ralph looked very carefully over the edge of the cliff. Very carefully he sized it up.

"I won't need a wrecker cable. Or your hook. I'll go on down there. Fetch her back myself."

Actually the path was pretty wide. The deputy was careful. The paramedic in a white jacket followed along.

They pried her out of the wedge, sort of one piece at a time.

She was limp, but the paramedic called up and said she was breathing good.

This Deputy Ralph carried her back up the path to the white sheets of the stretcher. Very smoothly, they slid this Hauk girl inside the ambulance, and I handed the paramedic her big Mexican purse.

We all drove to the County Hospital, and probably the wrecker man ended up with the Fifth of Buckmeister Springs.

Anyway, looking back on it:

She's still beyond the Pass, beyond Grass Valley, in a County Facility—one of the best. Some of that night exposure went into pneumonia; antibiotics did the job. Also some upper-vertebrae involvement. She is still in a coma, though every time she responds to her name.

Anyway, looking back on it:

I told Ralph the Deputy everything he needed for his report, as follows:

This Miss Hauk had the map to her friend's— unknown to me—A-frame mountain get-away type of cabin. She was bringing Hi-Protein to this dog. Mostly I volunteered my Pontiac, a few quarts of oil, and was mainly her driver. Because of her faulty map, however, we arrived a little late, after dark—and no dog.

Being worried very much about the dog, we stayed on. For sure I couldn't say when she left the A-frame for the Pontiac, me being sound asleep at the time because of the rain. Or, I presumed she was sleeping in the car to stay dry which was all right with me because we didn't have no relationship.

Ralph the Deputy, and the two doctors, and the paramedic seemed to have no trouble with that—maybe because I was still wearing sandals.

But: either to visit the Ladies Room, or she forgot and opened the wrong car door, *or* she walked around in *front* of the acacia bush, the night being rainy and I guess very dark . . .

"Was that Hi-Protein in the Fifth I saw on the ledge?" Ralph the Deputy asked me.

"Yes," I said. "She mentioned it was a Long's special. Maybe as an afterthought she was bringing it back to the A-frame. What we had there was two six-packs I bought coming up, at Quoit Junction. I know it's a tragedy, and I'll never know what happened in the Pontiac. But I do know she was herself: she locked everything.

"It could have been worse, much worse," the older doctor said, and that seemed to wrap it up for all concerned. I never did sign anything.

Except for one thing: who pays?

What I said was as follows:

Being mainly her driver on this trip, I did not know all that much about Miss Hauk's background, or her next-of-kin. I understood, however, there was some family in Illinois, and her father was a welder. I presumed information in the big Mexican purse was their best bet.

I was using my head: what they wanted was Merriweather *off* their County Rolls. But if she remained anonymous, a Jane Doe, then she would still get comparable, adequate treatment. When she came out of it, I could ask her in private how much she wanted her folks to know. In California, when the State *and* the County gets involved, don't move too fast.

To get Lou-Robin's sleepbag, and also to kick all the soup cans and empty supplies off the deck in case Ralph the Deputy came back to search for an address, I drove back to the A-frame just briefly. I left the motor running. No dog, so I dumped his Hi-Protein into the bushes. If hungry enough, he would find it.

Without pushing it, much later that same night, I hit Tampico #2: under the wire for a Triple-back. Two days later, after I was fully rested, I returned Lou-Robin's sleepbag and told Lou-Robin about Merriweather and how when I found the dog he just bolted into the underbrush.

All this happened six months ago.

At first I telephoned quite a few times. The Community Hospital desk always said this: "Guarded condition" and, "Yes. Every time she responds to her name."

Now I think less about it, which is understandable for Time is a Great Healer.

Many times I wished we had met sooner because with no trouble at all I could have got her on SSI. As a girl, once, she had a seizure, probably an epileptic seizure, and with two witnesses; with good papers she could have been on Social Security Supplemental Income today.

As for dog, I guess wilderness is his philosophy.

–Hey, Lou-Robin! Hit the long Ball!

–And no salt. Salt on the rim of a glass will kill you.

The Confessions
of Friday

Those Island memories of order and innocence fade
now with my waning sexuality and from the increased
burthen of this, my Public House.

Sole proprietor of this Flute & Cobbler, my mir-
rored, well-lighted cubicles above-stairs for your pleasures, without rancor, and now called Jas. Friday, I live
on. Even so, I understand an Island held now only in
memory, held while ironshod carriage wheels outside
echo in the fogs of the Thames and then re-echo along
the stone alleyways of London, well signifies the True
Nature of our lives.

It is almost winter, past noon; my accounts are to-
date, my desk lamp burns. In the centre of a lamp's
flame again, I see the sun rise in those savage latitudes
of the River Oronoque. Once I lived there. I elected to
depart.

All the more odd: his storybook, his so-called novel,
his *Life and Strange Surprising Adventures of Robinson
Crusoe, Mariner York* is still believed, is still read by certain Gentlemen. For those perversions, I hold one Defoe,

Dissenter, sometimes Sectarian Preacher, solely responsible. The man's a scoundrel, an opportunist: he dare not set one foot in my Flute & Cobbler.

About that footprint. My own footprint discovered in the sand.

Oh, that footprint is now most celebrated, is said to be a "high moment in our literature." In fact, one day past noon, in the sand by the water's edge, I arranged for Crusoe to discover it.

From the very beginning I was also on that Island, *our* Island.

R. Crusoe was the first man into the lifeboat after our ship wrecked in the great storm. The boat swamped and Crusoe was swept ashore. Commonly, it is said, Crusoe was saved by holding fast to a rock; I happen to know he was saved by a ship's plank, random in the seas.

But I, Jas. Friday, also came ashore in the blackest night buoyed only by the wave's force to which I abandoned myself without either thought or plan—for such was my nature. I held no rock; I rode no plank. Yet I, too, survived.

Continually, R. Crusoe bleats of "Providence" but that night our difference was only in degree, in the color of our skin. Our feet found identical salvation on sand. So I ask you: "Whose Providence?"

Here are the facts. Judge for yourself.

Before dawn of that first day, already awake, I was cross-legged, facing East to watch the gigantic head and shoulders of the sun vault skyward to become the first dawn of this, my new, my liberated life. In wonder, I gazed across the illuminated swells of the sea. Through mists, intermittently, as though in a vision, I glimpsed the high stern, the wreck of the *Albion Castle;* in sunlight, in calmer seas, the ship was but two leagues offshore. I observed that wreck only as a distant curiosity.

Well refreshed by sleep, with no care for the future, I went singing along the beach. The tide incoming filled my footprints as I walked.

Beyond the next point of land, I discovered one Robinson Crusoe.

I bent closer, the better to see Crusoe's face.

In this day's first heat, his body and his bodyrags gave off an offensive odor. As Crusoe breathed, he seemed to sink deeper into the sand. One unnaturally white, exposed arm still clutched a ship's plank; by contrast, my own black, naked arm was supple, alive. For one moment I feared this man.

Aboard the *Albion Castle* (6 guns, 14 men), Crusoe was not well respected. In storms he was pious, but in good weather bullied all persons of "lower" social order than himself. Because I was black and our dear Captain's boy (slave), Crusoe did not conceal a malevolence towards me and all my kind.

Treacherous, a hardened seafarer, once a captive of the Moors, Crusoe boasted incessantly of profits taken from voyages past. On his trowser belt, Crusoe carried always his knife in a leather sheath. With satisfaction, I saw this identical sheath still in place, now filled with sand.

My moment of fear passed as the shadow of a gull's wing skims the sand: my emotions were neither long nor very deep, for such is my nature. To kill Crusoe where he lay did not cross my mind; instead, I was overwhelmed with joy to know we were now equals, were not alone on this desperate Island. R. Crusoe was now my fellow-man: with that clear recognition, the final vestige of slave-mentality passed from my life.

Flies buzzed at Crusoe's eyelids. For the joke of it, for play, I dribbled a handful of sand near the fly-blown mouth.

Crusoe twitched. Violently, he rolled his head. In sleep Crusoe called out for his mother.

I departed. On a low dune, not thirty feet above him, I blended into the vines, the leaves. An audience of one, as though looking down into a sunlit theatre, I observed R. Crusoe, Mariner York, awake.

Crusoe shook my sand from his beard, his hair, from his rags; he stooped on all-fours, then stood erect.

Crusoe walked a few paces one way, then another, as though still confined to a ship's deck. He raised both arms to Heaven, stared briefly into the tropik sun. Overly long, he gazed across the now-calm sea: in a slanting ray of the sun, glistening off-shore like a jewel in the black fist of the reef, Crusoe saw the wreck of the *Albion Castle* (120 tons; 14 men). As he watched, entranced, a long comber broke as spray across the bulwarks of that wreck.

Crusoe cried out. He called each name of the fourteen (white) crewmen; he shouted for Van Dryssen, our old Dutch Captain, lately my dear master. No one answered.

Behind me, surprised by that hoarse, strange voice, a massive flock of sea birds rose flapping.

Crusoe kneeled in sand, sobbed as a child. With the hectoring voice of the bully, Crusoe prayed. Neither sea nor sand nor sea birds made reply.

At that moment of unrequited silence, I felt great compassion for R. Crusoe, Castaway.

Finally, Crusoe turned his back on the sea. He stood not twenty paces from where I lay among vines.

From fern leaves and fronds, Crusoe fashioned a conical hat; he placed it on his head as protection from the sun. Savagely, he broke down a small tree, and got himself a staff, a walking stick. With his new hat and cane, and with new determination, Crusoe turned again to the shore.

I laughed and laughed: Crusoe had walked along my own footprints in the sand, footprints which lead directly to my place of hiding. But Crusoe saw them not. Being now castaway by "Providence," Crusoe saw himself as utterly alone; therefore, he saw and could see only those things which confirmed his new role.

The sun was directly overhead. I gathered a few berries within reach. In the first hot hours of the day, I felt my natural indolence assert itself; I felt myself become at one with the rhythm, with the life of another Island, an order of things felt but not seen.

Towards evening I awoke. Crusoe was gone.

I remembered the savagery with which Crusoe attacked the defenseless tree to get him a walking stick; therefore, I was at pains to keep from his sight. I became a shadow moving through the undergrowth, so quiet even shore birds fed undisturbed.

Not far from the place Crusoe had prayed in the sand, I found a pile of things he had gathered on a long beach-patrol. He had arranged this debris in a precise order: three hats, one cap, and two shoes which were not fellows. Crusoe's rude monument signified the end of my dear Captain, his crew, and of their enterprise to take slaves in Africa.

More important, Crusoe was now returning from his first trip to the wreck of the *Albion Castle*.

From the bush above a small inlet, I watched Crusoe's new raft run aground on a sandbar beyond the mouth of the creek. The raft was made of ships spars, was cumbersome—and loaded with goods.

With his stick, Crusoe tried to free the raft and its cargo. Then with a boat hook from the wreck, he punched violently at the water. He cursed. In desperation, Crusoe finally jumped overboard. Without his weight, the raft unexpectedly broke free of the sand. Wind and tide at once pushed his raft back towards the ocean.

Crusoe swam in chase. He managed to catch the end of a line which bound the ship's spars. Crusoe knotted the line around his shoulders. Steadily he swam. Then, hysterically, he threw his arms at the water—made no headway. Crusoe became weaker, gave up. He tried to regain the low-riding raft but was too weak. Raft and man drifted steadily seaward.

I stood. I was at the point of rescuing Crusoe, our raft, and our first cargo from the *Albion Castle*.

Whereupon an afternoon inshore breeze came up. Our raft began to drift once again towards the inlet. Crusoe was strong enough to guide the raft, but not more. In half an hour, man and raft drifted ashore about twenty yards below me. Exhausted, Crusoe lay himself athwart our "goods," more dead than alive.

I waited, concealed, until Crusoe slept.

For the second time that day I observed Crusoe snoring.

Again, I might have killed him, but—childlike—was eager to see the goods which Crusoe fetched us from the wreck:

. . . One chest carpenter's tools. Four pieces dried goat's flesh. One Dutch cheese, rind broken. Four demijohns Cordial Waters. Most fearful: two pistols, two large powder horns, one bag shot; two fowling pieces; also two swords, handguards rusty. The twenty powder kegs aboard were still dry and waited in the reared aft-cabins.

Closely I inspected this mixed cargo. I liked the Cordial Waters and one cheese with a broken rind; the iron things, the armament, I understood not at all.

And, of course, I saw it very well. While I slept, Crusoe labored: from piety he had gathered the debris of the dead, including two shoes not fellows; that done, he had risked his life to gain the wrecked ship on the reef. For that risk had got him two swords, pistols, shot, powderhorns, fowling pieces.

Then, sadly, I understood: early we two had been free, innocent; this Island, this new world had been before us. With fowling pieces ashore, however, Crusoe need place one hand on his pistol and once more I became a slave, his slave.

Alone, Crusoe severed our natural dependency, one man upon the other. In so doing, Crusoe divided our Island unequally: my island against His Island. These things I saw, but held no hard feelings: if to be armed was Crusoe's nature, our stay on this Island was only beginning.

Therefore, I turned away, deserted Crusoe where he slept.

I walked south along the water's edge, and the tide closed my footprints.

At a distance, abruptly, I turned East. My half of this Island lay across an interior spine of hills. Wind among stones taller than my head made the noise of wild beasts; as I walked more quickly, even the ferns hissed. I was a dark shadow in motion through dark hills.

At dawn, I emerged from trees. I saw our Island's other shore, there to live in ways most suited to my nature.

II

Without plan, without thought, each season passed, each season's end marked by the bloom and the decay of a bush-like yellow flower. Twice each year rain became incessant, went then back to the sea. My half of the Island was a paradise of innocence; here time itself was lost, for I neither changed nor seemed to grow older. Of Crusoe, of his schemes, I gave no thought. Each night, overhead, the Southern Cross swung low in steady orbit.

Two years passed.

Each tree held parrots, their wings blue and orange among green leaves. Fish entrapped themselves in tide-pools, and when I stooped to see my own reflection in the water, of curiosity, the fish swam into my hands. I saw ground hares, pigeons, tortoise, and goats with their young; yet, with berries sweet in all seasons, with food everywhere, I took only tortoise eggs or fruit. I neither fished nor stored meats against famine; I killed no living thing and yet that land fed me.

Four years passed.

Of clothing, I had none. My skin turned dark in summer, became less so in the two seasons of rain when I slept much among fronds in my dry cave. By chance one day, I covered my body randomly with wet, scarlet leaves. As I lay in the sun, I felt the wet leaves suck my skin. When I removed the leaves, my skin was bleached in leaf-patterns of white. I was delighted. For days, I covered my body with leaf-shapes. By arranging small leaves on my skin, I came to resemble a vine, a pal-metto, or even the shell of a tortoise. Decorated artfully, I blended perfectly with flowers. At last my blackness was nullified. I became all things, a creature without qualities.

And I was young, my sexuality not yet waning. When the impulse seized me—which was often—I vis-ited one of my six forked tree branches, all at least thirty feet above the ground. These forks I lined with moss, then laved them with wildbee honey. These treeforks I embraced. In ecstasy I tossed wildly in the seawinds. I reached climax. Then I slept while the breeze rocked both the sweet, moss-lined fork and my limp body. . . .

Eight years passed.

One day at noon, my skin dappled, I rose from sleep among the yellow flowers, those blossoms already decayed, for this was a season's end.

Offshore, all in a row, coming rapidly towards me, I saw five *canoes*. They converged. The black oarsmen leaped out; they beached the hulls. Only then, on the breeze, I heard the voices: the shouts of savages—what? Come to take me?

Forty-one spear-armed men at once began to work: one group dug a deep hole in the sand; others ran the beach to get firewood. In headdress-feathers and calico, their drums beating a slow frenzy, the chiefs of this war party danced on one foot around and around the hole in the sand.

A single, wood-gathering savage came inland, paused not ten paces away; he was five feet three or four inches in height, a white animal bone skewed through the nose; the forehead, cheeks, arms, and smooth, perspiring chest were tattooed most intricately with purple dye. My own skin blended perfectly with the yellow flowers. The fearful savage walked on.

Their fire on the beach burned brighter. Soon the blacks circled around and around two men whom I had thought were motionless priests. Then I understood: the two moved not, because they were bound with ankle cords.

From behind, without warning, the two bound men were struck. Fell. Were killed instantly by warclubs.

I watched. Fascinated, the black savages cut out the guts, then cut off the heads, the arms, the limbs, all the while shouting with joy.

When that awful meat was broiled, they ate. Last, and apparently with especial relish, they passed, one to the next, the two roasted hearts. Each savage—without reluctance—ate his cooked share.

If fascinated, I was also sickened. If motionless, I was also relieved. They did not yet know of my presence— or did they? Continuously, four dogs, tied by ropes to the canoes, lunged and barked in my direction.

The blacks were a war party. They had taken two prisoners. But when not at war, at some precise phase of the moon, would they return for me? I presumed so.

My only thought was flight.

Through those next hours, I trembled beneath palm fronds in my cave. Incessantly, I thought of Robinson Crusoe. I saw myself warning Crusoe of savage boat crews, of their dogs lunging at the underbrush; I would throw myself at his feet, give myself to him, claim him my protector—for such was my nature.

Dawn turned my cave's mouth purple, then orange. I rose, and at once ran away between tall rocks, ran west beneath thwarted trees.

Past sunrise, after eight years of innocence, again I saw the austere, rocky coast of Crusoe's Island. The inlet and the creek below had not changed; on the distant reef no sign remained of the *Albion Castle*. All was quiet, as though his half of the Island were suspended in the early morning sunshine between sky and sea.

I heard gunshots.

The noise of a fowling piece re-echoed from a nearby gully.

I heard the cries of sea birds, the panic of wings beating. Crusoe was shooting his breakfast.

Cautiously, I walked towards the noise: because Crusoe's guns were in order, I was less afraid.

Suddenly I drew back. My vine-leafed skin blended perfectly with the underbrush.

Crusoe was walking this same path, not twenty paces away.

Crusoe wore a conical, peaked hat of the whitest goatskin, the rim broad against the tropik sun. Over each shoulder was a fowling piece. From Crusoe's belt hung one of the swords, its handguard now brightly shining; his doublet and trowsers were of fine skins. On his belt, I saw the sheath of leather, a knife snuggly fitted, its handle of shaped horn. From his gun barrels hung four birds, maimed, bleeding.

Sturdy, stooped, a little fat, Crusoe came towards me. His face and his expressionless blue eyes thrust forward beneath the conical hat, as though he were moving at great speed. Crusoe loomed large, then passed my bush—an apparition in goatskin.

In eight years, I had seen no other person. And oh, I felt a great rush of affection for I was Emotion's child.

Yet I hesitated, drew back: if Crusoe and his guns signified my protection, those things also signified oppression, the shackles of iron, the color of my skin.

Therefore, in the weeks ahead, from vines, from aloft in trees, at times standing not ten paces away, I observed Robinson Crusoe's every move. At sunup he arose, kneeled in prayer; daily he importuned—or threatened—a God who had either saved or had abandoned him. Prayers done, Crusoe talked aloud to himself all the day, a habit engendered by his own years of isolation. At first I enjoyed the sound of his voice: to me it was a half-remembered human music.

Unwittingly, inevitably, Crusoe told me everything: his present fears, his future plans for his New Order in part already imposed upon these stones. If Crusoe was

his own Grand Architect, sole audience, and only con-
sumer, he was at the same time both devious and cunning. If Crusoe's life was predictable and boring, I also
laughed to observe him set little deadfalls and security-
traps which he, himself, then must remember and later
avoid. On his side of our Island, everywhere, there were
now monuments to his intellect, his industry.

Central to Crusoe's New Order was The Cave. Here
his wealth was stored. With its corridors, its propped,
dug-out rooms, The Cave was at the Island's highest
point. Often when Crusoe was at hunt, I, too, avoided
his elaborate little traps. I, myself, constantly explored
his most sacred cave.

Beyond his storerooms I came upon a startling, iso-
lated, cubicle: here was Crusoe's clepsydra, his water-
clock. This ingenious, altar-like construction was a glass
demijohn from the wreck, the glass pierced artfully to
allow water, drop by drop to escape into a bowl of brass.
By trial and error Crusoe had marked the bowl with
Roman numerals. All through the days and nights the
water drop-dropped, and in this way Crusoe had mas-
tered Time, had contained it.

A connected, adjacent room was Crusoe's "Academy
of Weights and Measures." Here he had contrived the
measure of an inch, a foot, a yard, a rod; likewise, a gill,
a pint, two pecks, a gallon, a dram, and one pound
avoirdupois. All models were of laboriously polished
granite or the hardest of cured woods. These artifacts
I understood to be the instruments, the weapons, of
reason.

Deeper in The Cave, connected and reached by short
tunnels, were Crusoe's "Court of Justice," and its nearby
jail. By chance, later, I discovered a trap door, and a
smaller, deeper chamber. Here Crusoe had built a rack,
stocks, and a modest gallows; also, with less care, he had

assembled a brutally heavy, crude cross of oak. At these things, and more, I stared in wonder.

Well enough, however, I understood these monuments were crude extensions of Crusoe's logical, mercantile, ranging mind. Moreover, these things were most surely built against the day another storm wreck of mariners or slaves *en route* from Africa might come ashore to populate Crusoe's imagined "kingdom."

Well enough, also, I understood myself to be Crusoe's best chance to get him at least one citizen—albeit black—to govern.

In the domestic reaches of The Cave, I viewed rude bags of seed grains, dried goat's meat on hooks; tools, weapons, two chests, fine clothes; one chest, gold.

The gold I marked well, but saw no way to get it for myself.

Into what I believed to be The Cave's deepest reach, Robinson withdrew for solace, for meditation. In a soundless chamber, lined with pillows, an intricate woven canopy overhead, in this dark place which was so feminine, so maternal, Crusoe allowed but two furnishings. On the one hand was an altar and the Bible, a relic of a ship once wrecked on that distant reef. On the other hand, in the centre of a ring of pillows, was an elaborate Hookah, an intricately constructed water pipe. Once each month, Crusoe allowed himself to smoke one ounce of his precious, remaining tobacco.

This dark, clandestine, room—and the Hookah pipe—at once became my obsession. While Crusoe repaired his irrigation system for the rice paddies or sorted and numbered his goats, all through the hottest hours of every possible day, I came here. Without restraint, greedily, I smoked Crusoe's precious tobacco. I liked to watch the changing shapes, the patterns of my smoke as it rose to the ceiling of the caves. All ashes, all evidence, I swept carelessly into what I presumed was a well in the corner of the room.

Then one day, bored, careless, under the influence of the rising coils of smoke, I lay alone in the centre of this most feminine of chambers. I slept.

Suddenly I awoke. I heard the clatter of deadfalls, of gates, of a goat herd bleating.

Crusoe was here: had returned unexpectedly. A summer storm—and lightning—was driving him headlong into our Cave.

Terrified, I picked up the water pipe. I threw the Hookah, lighted, into the well.

I crouched. I ran on all fours along the chamber walls. I was trapped.

Eyes half-closed from rain, half-blinded by lightning, Crusoe could not see clearly.

We passed, almost touched in the corridor. If he half-glimpsed me, Crusoe believed I was a goat.

Sideways, I threw myself into the jail-room.

At that moment fourteen barrels of gunpowder exploded.

And orange, livid flame rushed like an orange wind from The Cave.

Crusoe seemed to lean forward into the flame. Then in midair he was lifted up, thrown back, as though hurled from a cannon. I saw him outlined: a flapping ragdoll against The Cave's mouth.

Deeper in The Cave, I heard timber-props and walls let go.

Because I was in The Cave's most protected room, I lay unharmed. I ran for the entrance. Behind me, coming closer, I heard slabs of rock coming down. . . .

I understood: when I threw away the Hookah pipe, it landed not in a well but in Crusoe's powder magazine.

Outside, blown clear of The Cave's mouth, I found Robinson Crusoe.

I bent above his singed, smouldering beard. Clothing asunder, not conscious, Crusoe curled on the mossy roots of a rubber tree as though in sleep.

I felt great remorse. Oh, so very much, I regretted my sloth, my aimless self-centred life which led to this wanton destruction. For the pleasure of watching rings of smoke, I had obliterated Crusoe's labors, his dreams of governance. His beard still smouldered. I poured water on his poor, flame-ravaged face.

About me I saw two split baskets, two muskets, their barrels twisted; the Weights and Measures now rubbish; his Calendar Mast on fire; two goats burned terribly and crying; garments burning, two split sacks of rice. And over everything, the industrial, knife-sharp odor of gunpowder.

And yet, Crusoe breathed.

To give Crusoe new hope, to redress the wrong I had done him, to reform my life, to make amends, the very next day I watched until Crusoe waded into the saltwater of the sea to treat his powder burns. When Crusoe was waist-deep in water, as he stared with longing at an empty sea, I walked openly to the beach, to the shoreline.

Knowing well that in this dazed, timeless state, he must now observe it, must be astounded, knowing well he must now embrace me as an equal, I left that single—and that now *so* famous—footprint in the sand.

Crusoe came ashore.

As I had arranged from the beginning, Crusoe stared, then shouted for joy.

Crusoe fell to his knees in prayer, and I stood beside him.

I placed my hand on Crusoe's shoulder.

At the touch of my hand, Crusoe turned, saw me. Despite his ruined, blackened face, Crusoe almost smiled.

"You . . . You!" he said, for to Crusoe's mind I was not so much a person as I was his own prayers answered.

If at that moment Crusoe thought I was a savage, a mindless thing, I was also a man.

"You," Crusoe said. Then he strengthened. In his old voice of command he said:

"I name you . . . Friday. James Friday."

And so I have been called to this very day.

III

Of my life with Crusoe those next eight years, little more needs be said. If Crusoe built first an elaborate, rational empire in his own image, he now felt the advancement of age. But I was young, so he unleashed upon me his intellect, his old obsessions. We became teacher and pupil. I did not resist.

Our new work was to exhume the ruined Cave, to retrieve the fragments of his ruin. Each day we labored. Our first goal was to recover, intact, Crusoe's chest of gold. Whereupon, I was paid wages in gold, first at the apprentice and then at a journeyman rate. In the end, all gold was mine, and Crusoe paid without remorse.

Of my education, always after working hours, first came language. I pretended to know not one word of English; therefore, Crusoe "taught" me first these words: *Father, Son, Sin, Hell, Good Works, Salvation, Apocalypse.* Crusoe was amazed that I spoke English fluently—and so soon. To teach me to read, Crusoe wrote first letters, then words, and then his memory of biblical passages on the sand of the beach. Soon, I could write a fair hand, could do sums quickly.

Being austere, Crusoe rejected my convenience of moss-covered tree forks laved with honey; because of his example, I too came to find this practice boring and yet my sexuality did not wane. Therefore, one night during the incessant spring rains, deep in our palmy, frond-lined cave, I lay down beside Crusoe. I placed my head upon his chest—and he stiffened where he *lay*. Then my lips played lower along his body until my breath pastured across his belly—and more. Yes, and more.

Oh, at first that thing between us was rude. Artfully, however, I showed Crusoe other more exotic things not learned by a common sailor, even on his longest voyage. In the end, well pleased, Crusoe accepted our life for what it was.

In the end, I worked no more. Instead, I played all day, made kites, caused feathers to float long distances on the afternoon breeze, slept much in warm, curved stones on the beach—for such was my nature.

This indolence also came to an end, not by the return of black savages, but by a white speck on the horizon. The speck became a topsail schooner, flying the colours of His Britannic Majesty, Captain Beam, *The Huntress*, of Bristol.

"What," Robinson Crusoe said, when the first boats landed to take on water, "what, sirs is this year?"

"Why it's the year 1716. And why do you ask?"

With the water aboard, with my intention privately (and I felt almost passionately affirmed) by Captain Beam, with a chest of gold now rightly mine, I deceived Crusoe.

At the time, of course, I knew he would have had it no other way.

In the dead of night, before the first rays of the sun, I rowed me in a small boat, and quietly boarded *The Huntress*. Because I had gold—and for other more personal reasons—I shared the Captain's quarters.

We sailed for England with the tide.

Yes, Crusoe remained alone on his Island; and if alive is there to this day—for such was his nature. The choice was rational; almost certainly he wished it so. In all candor, however, if I ever think of Crusoe, it is without affection.

This desk lamp burns low. The first dark noises of another winter rumbles like carriage wheels through the streets of London.

My Flute & Cobbler is snug—and paid for with gold.

My accounts are to-date.

This other Island, this England, is now my home; this publik house is now my castle.

And who shall say I did not thus escape Crusoe's terrible dreams of Empire?

The War in the Forest

For Andrew Lytle

That winter in a forest where for days no sun came through the fog, where snow drifted against the trunks of trees, where metal—a tire iron, the knife, a machine pistol—burned the skin from our hands, where the Germans held snow-camouflaged log bunkers, their tree-burst mortar shells and a man cut down by a hurled tree limb lay in the snow while we squatted, saw ice form in a dead man's nostril; at that time in the winter forests of Alsace, we held no prisoners.

Germans surrendered or were captured; Americans also surrendered or were captured. But for nearly a month we shot and the Germans shot all prisoners. Our understanding.

Our 17th was a combat team, a loose functional outfit with the usual misfits.

We had few topo maps, but we did have ammunition, the morphine sterrettes stolen from medic packs, brandy or cognac in our canteens, a few anonymous, white, new-issue parkas. That winter our platoons were much under strength, somewhere in Alsace, sometime in December.

The German platoons opposite were even more under strength, always with an older sergeant, a good corporal, the others young, in fact, boys.

They had less ammunition, no fuel, worse boots. Their supply line was short, their maps and local knowledge good, for other German troops had held this terrain a very long time. All summer their engineers concealed *shu* mines, Bouncing Bettys, land mines, trip wires now covered with snow. Those engineers were gone; their replacements came here from the Eastern fronts, the survivors of winter in Russia.

Neither side had men for additional guard duty, MPs, Battle Police, or a stockade. Neither side had a man to march prisoners back. So we shot prisoners in this way:

–Sergeant, march them back. Our regular route.

–Yes, Sah, and a Sergeant always yelled, *Heraus!*

Our *Wermacht* prisoners, helmets gone, cold, eyes exceptionally bulged in their sockets as though the skin were frozen white on their skulls, always formed a line. Their older Sergeant knew what was up; the boys sneered, no doubt believed they had again survived.

Then five or six prisoners got prodded along, hands on the top of their heads, disappeared all in a row into the forest.

Out of sight, then off the path, then deeper in the forest drifts, those of us who knew to listen heard short bursts of an automatic pistol, his grease gun. Later the Sergeant reported in:

–Sah, they runned. So I got off some rounds.

–Sergeant, only thing to do. So forget it.

Those of us who understood "regular route" also understood the Sergeant first made them lie down. That way he avoided six single shots—something a Chaplain under oath might later recall.

As though craftsmen in the same line of work, the Germans did almost the same thing with us, their prisoners, for we found men all in a row we knew very well, face down in a snow drift. They, too, were shot, but always with one bullet through the head as though a *Waffen* SS sergeant or officer had not much ammunition. There was, however, one difference.

These things when our fighter bombers were grounded for weeks by silent, dense fog.

II

As a Colonel in Division Headquarters or a later historian might view it, our war was stalemate and therefore became the Order of Battle, a Summary of Casualties, MIAs, Significant Excerpts from Interrogation.

To us, however, everything except the cold and the forest and the snow became personal, almost domestic. We knew the enemy and they knew us.

At that time I was a Warrant Officer (Reconnaissance) attached, but not assigned, a specialist in terrain, maps, gun emplacements; by rank neither a commissioned officer nor an enlisted man, not accepted wholly by either.

At age twenty-three, outwardly, I was a loner: field-smart, resourceful, a neck-scarf of red silk. Emotionally, I was about sixteen; more than anything I wanted to stay alive and to belong, for tomorrow, or another tomorrow, I expected in some way to be killed and no one at all, no one, would remember either that moment or my circumstance. I had stopped writing letters home to Ohio where I was born.

Emaciated, touchy, I wore tailored shirts, was a talker, always armed, was always secretly excited to hear the burst-of-five roll of automatic weapons firing unseen somewhere in that forest. At the same time I avoided men of rank, all Chaplains, believed deeply I lived without illusions, at a distance admired The Cajun.

So I was out before noon with Sergeant Brookshire to find some higher ground. Brookshire was also attached to the 17th with Quad-50 machine guns; his gun crews were always shooting at hawks. He wanted a more advanced gun position, maybe to get some real shooting.

The Sergeant stepped around a man-sized fir, much like a snow-covered Christmas tree.

In fact, I thought "Christmas tree" as Brookshire for one moment stopped mid-step, looked up—and his lower face blew away.

For one second his very new parka held him upright. Then he was down, one boot kicking and kicking the snow.

I rolled back, crouched behind a larger tree. No other sound, and nothing moved.

Upwind, probably from the crotch of a tree, a man called. To this day I am certain I heard it, in English:

—Red Scarf. I get you!

At that time I wore a red silk scarf, traded for cigarettes in a French dress shop. I was known; had a name.

I wanted to move. Could not move, not my boot, not my finger. I buried my face to conceal my own white breath-cloud.

Finally, I ran crouching deeper into the trees, headed back. After two hundred yards, I stopped, huddled in the snow to breathe.

Alone, parka-white in the fog among the fir trees, I drank cognac from my canteen, saw my leg and then my wrist begin to shake, but I was not now afraid.

I stood fully upright, went on in to report, and—worse—to tell Brookshire's gun crews.

Oddly, I began to laugh and laugh and said it first to myself and then said it out loud to the forest, with great elation said my outfit name: "Lucky Jim! Lucky Jim! Luck-ee Fuck-en Jim!"

In part my name came from my rank, always in the middle; in part it was a show-off, a gambler's name for someone sharp who again had come back when a good man like Sergeant Brookshire "stayed out" for by custom we seldom said a man had been killed.

I was alive, I was elated, and nothing else mattered; yet I knew others now would avoid me for here everyone was superstitious. The third time was the charm, so my luck had run out . . . beware the marked man.

Of course I was not superstitious, but I tried not to remember Brookshire; deeply I felt he had made some kind of error, so he got what he deserved. Later, morbidly, I thought more and more about our opposites, imagined vividly a man with a gun and a sniper's scope in a tree, looking down . . .

There were *Schutzstaffeln* (SS), a Battalion, the Death's Head Standard, once of Hitler's personal bodyguard, later *Waffen* (armed) SS. Their insignia was the *Totenkopf,* the Death's Head; even in the field a *Hauptsturmführer* wore his black uniform, the collar patch distinctive, his leather, black belt with the SS insignias.

Above all, an old-line Officer had the dagger in its black sheath, the blade embossed, *Meine Ehre Heitz Treue,* that blade, under oath, never to be surrendered. Those things were sinister and therefore highly prized; these things men sometimes died to possess. And the Luger, of course.

Now only the outward form of an SS elite remained; their replacements were not volunteers or "pure" of blood. Yet they were dug in and their *Oberscharführers* were cunning, lethal.

And we did shoot prisoners in our different ways.

We shot German prisoners with short bursts, the face up. Any head shot was through the forehead, that way helped identify a man found when the snows were gone, our "regular route."

When the SS shot us, it was face down, a massive single round into the back of the skull. That way blew off the frontal skull, the whole face. When found, when rolled over, our shock was the greater. In addition, time and place permitting, they cut off our fingers—to take high-school class rings.

Boston Bob and two others found Brookshire where I said: by then he was a block of ice, his parka gone. With a large safety pin—the sniper, no doubt—had fastened Brookshire's testicles to what remained of his upper lip—a frozen, grotesque, bulged-hair "moustache"—their play.

Quickly the word passed: "Asshole in our parka. Bring him in."

Brookshire's Corporal would personally take him our regular route—but more slowly.

For entirely different reasons, however, in pairs or alone at dusk, officers like The Cajun, or sometimes two sergeants, or occasionally an almost silent, withdrawn PFC, disappeared into the forest, went out on a personal recon, a long hunt.

Those men were gone sometimes one day, or three, and once The Cajun came in after four days—and then only to "re-up" it was said.

They hunted, stalked, a *Scharführer*, a sergeant, a "Scharfy." With great daring and patience, perhaps for a day and a night they might hole up within the sound of German voices; or, they ranged a long distance to take an officer—perhaps with driver and vehicle—at night, near a culvert.

About noon on the second or third day—unless he stayed out a man on recon returned, might display a wallet with children's pictures, an Iron Cross, German cigarettes, a Luger; Death's Head insignia, a black belt, or American high-school class rings. These things he sold to our replacements, but kept any SS dagger in its black sheath for his wife, back in The States:

> –Got me a ugly son-of-bitch of an Over Scharfy,
> a-taking his shit. Got his left eye
> at 260 yahds—some windage.

Men who very much liked a long recon became loners; eventually they stayed out, but not The Cajun. He had no other line of work.

By contrast my work even then was perhaps an older form, but still hanging on.

On random, late afternoons, an order might come down:

> *Out Recon, 18:00 hrs.*

I had a feel for those days, and nearly always had been wearing aviator glasses, avoiding bright light.

Corporal Scoofie, a German-speaking Syrian, said once to be of the New York mafia, "shaped" (as he said) with five others who preferred a recon to guard duty—irregulars.

In the supply tent we stood in a circle, our parkas not white, but of our own camouflage design. I checked each man; in turn they checked me: anything which might rattle, taped down; nothing at all to catch the light. Ammo; no rings.

At our outpost, each man whispered this day's Right Word, followed me to where a safe path ended, and only those who had used their stolen morphine were not afraid.

Now the temperature was minus zero, the snow exceedingly dry, and we became shadows moving then stopping and then moving again, keeping always to tree lines until I found higher ground and the trees thinned. For a minute overhead I saw the moon shine like beaten lead—dully—through the low clouds, was gone.

After one mile or more this ridge fell away towards a clearing. At its farthest edge, I saw rows of very large trees, but I did not go there.

On this higher ground above the clearing, I found a log well covered with snow. As had been understood at the onset, we lay down in a half-circle, our boots almost touching, each man facing a different sector, no two doped-up men together.

Silent, almost covered with blown snow, all around and overhead we heard only the wind among tree branches for one hour, then two.

My squad understood and I understood we were this night probably a "defensive" entry in a Field Report. Had there been tank or truck engine noises upwind, even very far away, we would hear them. Cowardice had nothing to do with it.

In some way, soon, I expected to die, but not for a report, not for some colonel's words on paper.

Finally, like snow men stiffly walking, we went back more closely together, back very much along our same trail—not good recon, but not mined—went back to the outpost where we began.

Mutt

And a voice somewhere in the dark, ahead, answered:

Jeff

In that way we came in, and once again in the supply tent no words were spoken.

The OD took my report and without changing expression cranked a field telephone:

Recon in; no contact.

For a long time I lay awake in my bedroll inside a shelter made of truck bows and what was once a small-wall tent, a lean-to covered with show. Because I could not prevent it, I saw again every shadow of this night, saw everything that next time might go wrong; yet, also, I saw the smoke-stack trees of this forest were like the shadows of an Ohio steel mill and my recon life was like the boy once on an Ohio farm who did not like but still yearned each Thursday evening for the lights, the band music, of a nearby market town.

At the time I was imaginative, but did not know it. Past three o'clock in the morning, as always, finally, I slept.

III

Two afternoons later, a new line of prisoners came in from the forest, their hands up.

We gathered around. I scented the curious odor of prisoners even in winter: feces, body odors.

Four German enlisted men; one officer. Our outpost had heard them a quarter-mile away. Half-blinded by the snow, half-frozen, not dressed for this weather, they stumbled past our guard, not ten feet from his post. The guard merely called ahead on his field telephone:

—Open the shit house door . . .

Scoofie of recon spoke German to the officer, a Captain.

Fuckin Quartermaster troops, Scoofie told us. Replacements. But assholes. Not okay physically.

I looked at the German captain: stooped, long neck, an Adam's apple. His blond hair was thinning; even in a field coat his chest was concave. His rimless, octagon, eyeglasses misted heavily. This one had schoolmaster written all over him. This one had done limited service for years at a Supply base. Then a someone declared him combat-ready for an SS outfit in the forest. But he never made it.

No one could find The Cajun, said to be in his bed-roll beating his dog.

This was Lieutenant Claggerd, an ROTC officer from LSU, once a highway engineer. The Cajun always referred to this winter forest as a "bye-you."

A loner, The Cajun was carried by the 17th from the Engineers, so Lieutenant Claggerd seldom reported to anyone. He had his own lean-to where he slept and stored his ammo and weapons.

The Cajun did only long hunts—and slept. Always he carried live grenades fastened to his shoulder straps. He liked very much his line of work: kill Germans and bring back trophies to sell.

Finally Lieutenant Claggerd showed up, helmet pushed back on his head, legs slightly bowed, smiling his turtle, man-eater, smile. He wore neither a ring nor a wristwatch. On the front of his helmet was a faded daub of white paint: First Lieutenant.

The Cajun walked once again around this bunch. He was armed with an issue .45, his Luger, a grease gun (machine pistol), and many ammo clips; his grenades were turtle shells hanging to his chest.

He glanced aloft: still enough light:

–Sah-jint. Take 'em back. Regular route.

–Sah! And a long-hunt sergeant took over: *Heraus* your asses!

There was also another form of things. Our sergeants shot German enlisted men; an Officer shot captured German officers. Something like having separate Clubs and latrines.

Abruptly, The Cajun turned to me, put his hands on his ammo clips, spoke loudly enough:

–And *Mister*—slurred in front of the non-coms:

–*You-all get Big Boy.*

The Lieutenant gestured towards their Captain:

–Mister, I'll *see* you take him. Regular route.

Scoofie understood, spoke German to the Captain and the Captain took two steps, reported almost formally to me. Someone in film or a moralist might say that precise moment was crucial, but it was not so.

I saw only the tops of trees. I saw a supply tent, two or three small-wall tents on packed snow; I saw little groups of men watching prisoners, and the final light of this day sliding down through the trunks of trees.

Smartly, GI, I answered the Lieutenant, The Cajun:

"Roger," pronounced *"Ra-Ja,"*

To the over-age-in-grade, stooped, Captain:

–*Heraus!*—*asshole.*

A line sergeant herded his German enlisted men all in a row to the far side of the clearing.

My .45 automatic came easily into my hand. I hit the butt end with my left palm, slammed home the clip. My German saw that, knew there was no round in the firing chamber.

This one was clearly relieved; now he was in charge of another officer.

The German's eye glasses had cleared. He was exhausted from his two days and a night lost in the forest, but now he could see.

I poked him once in the back with my .45, herded him towards another path to the south. As we entered the forest the tops of the trees disappeared, taken by a white, sliding mist.

The footprints of our path ended at the trunk of a tree.

The German stopped, turned to see if there were some mistake.

He heard the *snick-snack* of my gun's slide loading its round. With sudden, immense clarity that metal sliding told him something.

His mouth opened. He trembled first in his legs, then in his upper body. Standing roughly at attention in the snow, the forest all around, he could not believe. And then he did believe:

    –Frau, Frau. Kinder . . .

               –Gott.

When he raised his eyes towards the tops of the fir trees, I put the muzzle of the gun beneath his chin. Pulled the trigger.

For a moment he seemed to stand taller, on tip-toe. His head jolted back. He fell then into the snow.

He writhed, kicked once. There was no back at all to his head for now all of that was gone.

I turned, walked not quickly back along the path; the acrid smell of a .45 automatic recently fired seemed to walk with me, even after I put the gun in its leather holster hanging as always on my webbed belt.

Farther to the west, I heard faint, short bursts of a machine pistol: the sergeant, at the end of our regular route.

    –Made a break for it, I told The Cajun.

        –So I skinned him.

Lieutenant Claggerd pushed his helmet higher off his face, laughed at something. Ironically, humorously, only for the form of it, he said:

    –Mister, I *ain't* pleased. But you had a do it.

        –Now didunt juh?

That night I drank some of the cognac hidden in my bedroll. I was so exhausted my hand did not move when so ordered. Then I understood The Cajun's meaning: *"You had ado it."*

Had I said No, or hesitated, The Cajun would have shown me the way, and that way was deeper into the forest.

At a path's end, first The Cajun would have shot the German officer. And then shot me for if a man won't shoot a German, and especially a German officer, then you can't afford to keep the sonofabitch around.

And in those ways our war in the forest went on.

Much later, after The Cajun hooked up with another combat outfit and stayed out but was carried MIA, I saw it even more deeply: The Cajun did not like patrols to come in no contact; worse, when a Brookshire eats it, you shoot a sniper or a sniper ties your balls in a red silk scarf under your nose because you don't go out there to check.

And maybe it was not a sniper, maybe it was a German sergeant, a Scharfy, on his own long hunt.

IV

Past noon next day I awoke, came out into a light rain.

The entire 17th Combat Team was gone: Scoofie, Boston Bob, The Cajun. Too long in the woods, shot up, pulled back, gone. Because I was only attached (not assigned) no one remembered to wake me.

That did not matter for I was now attached to Ironsides, 22d Combat Team. Now I would have to do everything all over again, except new troops sometimes shoot each other after dark, and new officers at first would order daylight recons into the forest every day. Moreover a green outfit would attract German probes, night patrols in strength. Now one side or the other would shoot me; I saw this with a terrible clarity, understood this was so.

Ironsides was full strength, clean; every man had everything he was supposed to have. They chattered, shouted, told this forest they were new and they were here.

I found their Adjutant, a Major, who wore shining insignia on his hat, his collar, his parka, and who also had an overly large wristwatch with oversized black numbers—French.

He smiled a Texas A&M, ROTC, fullback's smile:

–Good lick, MacShit. Your ass is mine.

Just then with great longing, I remembered the 17th, even for that single moment when without illusion, wholly, I belonged: when The Cajun laughed and said, "You had ado it."

Because I was dried out by cognac, was hospital thin, they said I was just standing there on the snow, went limp, fell.

When I awoke, a medic was holding a mirror near my face, was reflecting his flashlight into my throat.

I saw my own face: not shaved, gaunt, very old, skin stretched tight across a skull, the eyes protruding as though to see beyond the mirror and more deeply into the trees . . .

–You're okay, the Medic Sergeant said.

    –No strep. Drink plenty of liquids.

In a few days the fog lifted and the sun seemed warmer than it was, especially towards nightfall.

With the sun our fighter bombers got off the ground, were silver and sunshine-metal flashing just above the tops of the trees. When I saw them going in, I felt suddenly elated, the grim joy of reprieve.

Only a few thousand yards away, muffled by the terrain and the woods and the snow now melting from every branch, I heard the first bombs, felt the earth beneath the snow shrug a little.

Almost overnight I became useless, an anachronism, for now the terrain ahead had new definition; our forward elements marked a target and with much newer radios called in the fighter bombers.

Even so, the Army can be intimate: the word passes, and some things everyone believes.

In a few days, with neither irony nor respect intended, the sergeants of Ironsides began to call me Lucky Jim.

I was someone aged but not old, a man still walking around, displaced, who each night slept in the canvas bows of a different truck: off the ground, ready to move out.

One day at noon, the forward elements of Ironsides entered and then moved easily through a clearing not mined at all.

Beyond, the terrain fell down and away to low hills, and then to a plain where there were fields, and barns, and houses, and no snow at all on crossed, black lines which were stone walls.

In this clearing, our fighter bombers had caught a German Field Headquarters.

Their dead horses lay where they reared or were running away when they died and were now beginning to swell. Field kitchens and dead men and trucks still burning, pay books, and boxes of ammo lay among fallen trees, as though something flooded this clearing, had flashed once, left only blue smoke, debris.

Because so many knew about a sergeant found with his balls pinned to his mouth—and his parka gone—and understood a Cajun officer was once behind the MLR for days but was now Missing In Action, a Communications Sergeant who once was a grade-school principal took me to the edge of this clearing to a downed tree. He thought I might want a souvenir.

The Sergeant showed me the dead German, this one wearing a slightly soiled, but still an American, white, parka stretched tight everywhere for he was beginning to swell.

The arm was raised, askew, elbow and hand raised as though hitchhiking. Someone from Ironsides, someone now a veteran, someone already on the plain already shooting inside barns and houses and over stone walls had cut off one finger, to take a class ring or a wedding band—something of value.

Looking back on it, very well I knew almost exactly what I was doing, or so it seemed.

But later they said in fact I fired and fired my Army issue automatic again and again into the belly and the chest and the face of a man dead between a log and boxes of ammunition. And not a real soldier: only someone in a Headquarters caught when a clearing was bombed.

They said I was trying to load another clip when a Supply Sergeant pinned my arms and I heard him call and call into the smoke:

–Medics, medics, medics . . .

The rear doors of a field ambulance opened, and after the needle's metal tip foraged into my skin, the doors of the ambulance closed and everything was dark.

After all those things, for a long time, I believed our war in the forest began and in all those ways at last ended.

But in fact, my war in the forest went on as it was at the onset, deeply I wished to belong but cannot belong even though I have tried to belong all the days of my life.

James B. Hall has authored or edited more than a dozen books of fiction, nonfiction, and poetry. An emeritus professor of literature at the University of California at Santa Cruz, he lives in Eugene, Oregon.